THE MEANING OF LIFE... AND OTHER STUFF

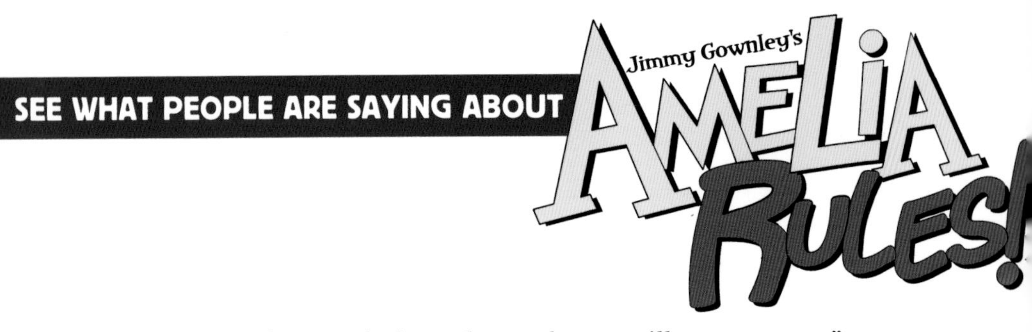

"Haven't read comics before? This is where you'll want to start."
—*Girls' Life*

"Perfectly captures the heartbreak, humor, and high drama of the middle school experience."
—Gene Yang, author of *American Born Chinese*

"Comic genius."
—GraphicNovelReporter.com

"I wish I could go back to middle school and make a friend like Amelia. I wish I could go back and *be* a friend like Amelia."
—the-trades.com

"So clever, smart, funny, and true. . . . This is one of the best graphic novel series out there for kids—and for adults with vivid, funny memories of childhood."
—Elizabeth Bluemle, the Flying Pig Bookstore

"One of the best cartoonists I know of, [Gownley] has never written a story that hasn't left me grinning madly."
—The Geeky Librarian

"Amelia Rules! remains my favorite graphic novel series for kids!"
—Tweendom.blogspot.com

"A Peanuts for the twenty-first century."
—*Comics Buyer's Guide*

"Simply one of the best all-ages comics I've ever seen."
—Mark Crilley, author/illustrator of the Akiko books

"Delightfully drawn and cleverly written."
—Orson Scott Card

"Side-splittingly hilarious. . . . Highly recommended for all ages and all libraries."
—*Library Journal*

"Full of wise-cracking jokes and quips, ingenious gags, screamingly funny dialogue, and the best of classic comic book antics."
—Megan McDonald, author of the Judy Moody series

"Amelia Rules! is . . . absolutely essential. Not only is it one of the finest comics of all time, it is one of the best examples of children's literature I have ever read."
—Kidz Corner Comic Reviews

"Smart and genuine."
—David Fury, writer/producer for *Lost* and *Buffy the Vampire Slayer*

"Inspiring and uplifting in ways that will make you want to stand up and cheer. . . . Here's hoping the series continues for a good long time."
—the-trades.com

"Amelia's family and friends will take up permanent residence in your heart."
—Bob Schooley and Mark McCorkle, creators of *The Penguins of Madagascar*

"Wonderful all-ages comic."
—*New York* magazine

"Gownley excels at putting a powerful message inside of a kid-friendly story."
—BSCKids.com

"Amelia Rules! . . . is a delightful entry for lovers of comics and realistic fiction. . . . She is a character to rival Ramona and Judy Moody."
—*School Library Journal*

"These kids are real . . . Gownley is a genius at capturing their perspective."
—ComicsWorthReading.com

MEET THE GANG!

Amelia Louise McBride:
Our heroine. Wise cracking, yet sweet. She spends her time hanging out with friends and her aunt Tanner.

Reggie Grabinsky:
A.k.a. Captain Amazing. Founder of G.A.S.P., which he forces . . . er, encourages, his friends to join.

Rhonda Bleenie:
Smart, stubborn, and loud. She wears her heart on her sleeve and it's filled with love for Reggie.

Pajamaman:
Never speaks. Always cool. His feetie jammies tell you what's on his mind.

Tanner:
Amelia's aunt and a former rock 'n' roll superstar.

Amelia's Mom (Mary):
Starting a new life in Pennsylvania with Amelia after the divorce.

Amelia's Dad:
Still lives in New York, and misses Amelia terribly.

G.A.S.P.
Gathering Of Awesome Super Pals.
The superhero club Reggie founded.

Park View Terrace Ninjas:
Club across town and nemesis to G.A.S.P.

Kyle:
The main ninja. Kind of a jerk but not without charm.

Joan:
Former Park View Terrace Ninja (nemesis of G.A.S.P.), now friends with Amelia and company.

Tweenie Zeenie:
A local kid-run magazine and Web site.

Atheneum Books for Young Readers
New York London Toronto Sydney

ATHENEUM BOOKS FOR YOUNG READERS
An imprint of Simon & Schuster Children's Publishing Division
1230 Avenue of the Americas, New York, New York 10020

Also available in an Atheneum Books for Young Readers hardcover edition
Book design by Sonia Chaghatzbanian
The text for this book is hand-lettered.
The illustrations for this book are digitally rendered.
Manufactured in China
0618 SCP
6 8 10 9 7
Library of Congress Cataloging-in-Publication Data
Gownley, Jimmy.
The meaning of life . . . and other stuff / [Jimmy Gownley]. — 1st ed.
p. cm. — (Jimmy Gownley's Amelia rules! ; 7)
Summary: While trying to figure out the meaning of life, Amelia learns that even when the world is scary and life is as mystifying as ever, some things, such as friends, do last.
ISBN 978-1-4169-8613-3 (hardcover) — ISBN 978-1-4169-8612-6 (pbk.)
1. Graphic novels. [1. Graphic novels. 2. Meaning (Philosophy)—Fiction.
3. Interpersonal relations—Fiction. 4. Friendship—Fiction.] I. Title.
PZ7.7.G69Me 2011
741.5'973—dc23 2011018407

SOME TIME AGO, IN PENNSYLVANIA...
AMELIA RULES!™
DO WE HAVE TO LET HER IN THE CLUB?

C'MON, RHONDA! AMELIA HAS PROVEN HER VALUE TO G.A.S.P.
AND WITH THE ADDITION OF—
WHAT WAS IT AGAIN?
"PRINCESS POWERFUL."
RIGHT. "PRINCESS POWERFUL"...
...COMPLETES THE G.A.S.P. TEAM.
OH, WE'RE FINISHED ALL RIGHT.
SHUT UP!
WORLD
ROCKER!

LOOK, IF WE'RE GOING TO BE A *REAL* TEAM, WE HAVE TO SWEAR OUR LOYALTY.
WELL, I'LL TELL YOU RIGHT NOW, I'M NOT DOING THE WHOLE "BLOOD BROTHER" THING.
BECAUSE *ONE:* I'M A GIRL.
TWO: I'M AFRAID OF POINTY THINGS.
AND *THREE*: I DON'T KNOW WHERE HER BLOOD HAS BEEN.
FINE. HOW ABOUT WE SPIT SWEAR?
EEEW! I DON'T KNOW WHERE YOUR SPIT'S BEEN EITHER!
WE'LL JUST PINKY SWEAR, OKAY?
THAT PART DOESN'T MATTER....
ALL THAT MATTERS IS THAT WE'RE IN THIS TOGETHER NOW...
...FOREVER...
...AND NO MATTER WHAT TRIALS, WHAT CHALLENGES, WHAT EVIL IS THROWN AT US...

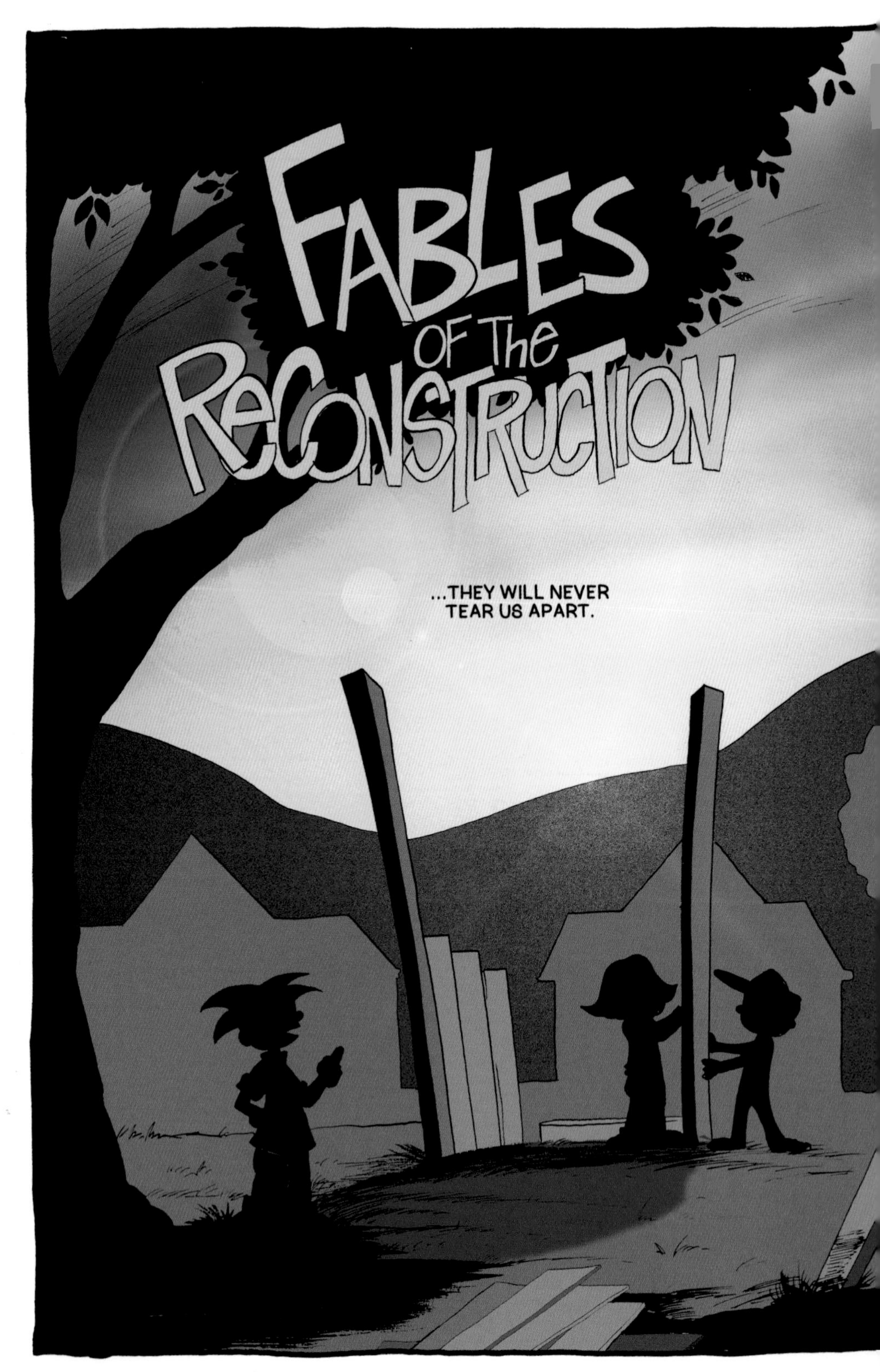
FABLES OF THE RECONSTRUCTION
...THEY WILL NEVER TEAR US APART.

YOU ARE LISTENING TO 96.5 WCTG-FM! CHINCOTEAGUE VIRGINIA'S FINEST ALBUM ORIENTED ROCK STATION.
JOINING US TODAY IS TANNER CLARK...
...WHO IS USING HER DAY OFF FROM OPENING FOR THE *GURLY GURLS*...
...TO ROCK THE PATRONS OF DON'S SEAFOOD RESTAURANT AND *LOUNGE*!
TANNER, THANKS FOR JOINING US THIS MORNING.
OH, MY *PLEASURE*!
WCTG 96.5 FM
The Eastern Shore's Album Music Source
SO, TANNER... ARE YOU READY FOR *FREAKY FREDDY'S FAB FIVE QUESTIONS*?
LET 'EM *RIP*, FRED MY MAN.
OKAY. HERE WE GO...

ON AIR
QUESTION ONE: WHAT IS THE GREATEST RECORD EVER MADE?
SGT. PEPPER'S LONELY HEARTS CLUB BAND.
QUESTION TWO: WHAT IS THE *WORST* RECORD EVER MADE?
THE SGT. PEPPER MOVIE SOUNDTRACK.
HA! OKAY, THREE: WHAT IS YOUR FAVORITE *FOOD?*
CAKE!
DRINK?
HMM... I LIKE THAT "LEMON ZINGER" TEA.
NICE! QUESTION FIVE—
WHO IS YOUR FAVORITE *SUPERHERO?*
NO CONTEST...
...PRINCESS POWERFUL.
PRINCESS POWERFUL?

HUH...
...NEVER HEARD OF HER.
Hmm... Mmm... Mmm...
WHHOOOAA...
GOOD JOB, GUYS!
REEEEEALLY NICE WORK!
IT'S LOOKING ALMOST AS BAD AS THE ORIGINAL!
LOOK, JUST TAKE OFF THAT STUPID CAPE AND GIVE US A HAND.
STUPID CAPE? I THOUGHT THIS WAS A G.A.S.P. MEETING. STUPID IS MANDATORY.
THIS IS A CONSTRUCTION MEETING, OKAY?
NOW, DO YOU WANNA HELP OR NOT?

AS AN EXPLOITED WORKER, I'D SUGGEST "NOT."
HEY!
BUT IF I HELP, WE CAN FORM A UNION!
AND STRIKE!
YEAH! POWER TO THE PEOPLE!
C'MON GUYS! THIS IS IMPORTANT!
THE CLUBHOUSE IS A SYMBOL OF OUR... UMM... YOUTH AND... FRIENDSHIP...
... AND Y'KNOW, JUNK LIKE THAT.
PLUS...
...YOU PROMISED.
SIGH
OH, BUHROTHER!
FINE.
WHAT DO WE HAVE TO DO?

C'MON, NOW!
HOIST IT!
HOIST IT!
HOIST IT!
REGGIE! Puff Puff I SWEAR...
Puff Puff IF YOU SAY "HOIST" ONCE MORE I'M GONNA BRAIN YOU!
WELL, I WOULDN'T HAVE TO SAY "HOIST..."
...IF YOU JUST WOULD HOIST!
FLUMP.
SPLAT
OH, NOW SEE? YOU DROPPED IT IN THE—
SPLOOCH
...mud.

JOAN, BY ALL THAT IS HOLY, I VOW TO AVENGE THIS SLIGHT TO MY HONOR. FROM NOW UNTIL I DRAW MY FINAL BREATH, PREPARE TO DEFEND YOURSELF, MADAM.
I LOOK FORWARD TO IT, SIR.
SIGH
HERE WE GO!
ACK!
OOOOOH! YOU'RE SOOOO
TAKE THAT!
HA!
MISSED ME! MISSED ME! NOW YOU GOTTA KISS ME!
SPAT!
WHIZ!
WHIZ!
UGH!
EEW GROSS!
YEAH! GROSS LIKE YOUR FACE!
BITE MY NOSE, SQUID BREATH!
HEH HEH.
SMOOSH
SQUELCH
SQUISH
SPLAT!
SPLOOSH

HEE HEE HEE
UHH...
SOMETHING FUNNY, CHUCKLES?
OH, I DON'T KNOW, I GUESS IT'S JUST...
THE ARGUING!
THE FIGHTING!
THE INSULTS!
IT'S NICE! IT REMINDS ME OF OLD TIMES.
HEY!
WHIP!
WHIP!
WHIZ!
OOOOOH!
YOU ARE SOOOOOO DEAD!

IT HAD BEEN A *REALLY* LONG TIME SINCE WE... I DON'T KNOW... ***PLAYED!*** AND I HAVE TO TELL YOU, I FELT LIKE A *KID* AGAIN. (YEAH, I KNOW I'M STILL A KID, I JUST FELT LIKE A *LITTLER* KID, Y'KNOW?)

ANYWAY... WE RAN AROUND LIKE NUTS AND HAD THE *BEST TIME*.
AND EVEN THOUGH WE WERE ALL TIRED AND LOOKED LIKE MUD-CAKED *WEIRDOS*...
... NO ONE WANTED TO GO HOME, SO WE ALL HUNG AROUND...
...AND JUST TALKED.

HEY, REGGIE, IF YOU DID GET SUPER POWERS, WHAT WOULD YOU DO?
ARE YOU KIDDING? FIGHT CRIME OF COURSE.
WHAM!
BIFF!
POW!
HA! YEAH, RIGHT!
SUUUURE!
WHAT?
I'M SERIOUS!
WELL, I—I MEAN, Y'KNOW, I GUESS IT WOULD DEPEND ON WHAT KIND OF POWER. BUT—
NO, IT WOULDN'T!
NO MATTER WHAT SUPER POWER ANY BOY GOT, HE'D USE IT FOR JUST ONE THING...
...TO SHOW OFF IN FRONT OF GIRLS!
THAT'S NOT TRUE!
OH, YES IT IS!
?

AND IT WOULD BE DOUBLY TRUE FOR REGGIE!
HEY, RHONDA.
SO, GET THIS... I WAS AT CHEERLEADING PRACTICE TODAY, AND —
WAIT! WAIT! WAIT!
DID YOU REALLY MAKE CHEER-LEADER!?
WOW! THAT'S AMAZING! AND YET YOU NEVER MENTION IT!
THAT WAS SARCASM, BY THE WAY.
YEAH. I PICKED UP ON THAT.
ANYWAY...
...WE WERE PRACTICING, AND I SAW REGGIE WATCHING US, RIGHT?
AND HE WAS STARING AT BRITNEY LIKE HE WAS HYPNOTIZED!
Shut UP. I was Not!
OOH! ANOTHER MALE FALLS TO THE EVIL POWER OF THE CHEERWITCH.
HEE HEE HEE.

RIGHT, SO ANYWAY...
UMM...
..., EXCUSE US.
YEAH, JUST HOLD ON A SEC-
WAHUH?!
HI.
ARE YOU GUYS G.A.S.P.?
WOOOOOOOSH!
THE GATHERING OF AWESOME SUPER PALS?

MAAAAAAYBE...
WHO'S ASKING?
WE.
ARE Y.I.K.E.S.!
WOOOOOOOSH!
YOUNG IMAGINATIVE KIDS EMULATING SUPERHEROES!
AND IF YOU ARE THE FAMOUS CAPTAIN AMAZING...
...THEN WE...
...ARE YOUR BIGGEST FANS!
WELL, IT'S ABOUT TIME!

YES, MY FRIENDS, THE BATTLES FOUGHT BY *THE GATHERING OF AWESOME SUPER PALS* WERE MANY.
BUT FROM THE *LEGION OF STEVES* TO *THE PARK VIEW TERRACE NINJAS* TO A FEW *UNFORTUNATE TEACHERS*, ALL OUR FOES HAVE BEEN *VANQUISHED!*
WHOA!

NOW DON'T GET ME WRONG, THESE VICTORIES WERE NOT EASY,
BUT THE HEROES OF G.A.S.P. WERE READY TO PAY THE PRICE TO PROTECT THE INNOCENT.
AND SO...
...EVEN THOUGH THERE WAS SOME LIGHT CHAFING...
...VIRTUE FINALLY TRIUMPHED!
BUT...

...BUT THE MONKEY WAS NEVER FOUND.
AND THAT'S HOW IT ALL GOT STARTED.
MONKEY?
WHOA!
EPIC!
OH, BROTHER!
HEE HEE!
DO YOU THINK WE SHOULD ASK ABOUT...
YOU KNOW!
PSSST PSSST... "SNEEZE BARF" PSSST PSSST...
OH NO!
I COULDN'T ASK ABOUT THAT ON THE FIRST DAY!
IT WOULD BE TOO OVERWHELMING!
IT WAS A PLEASURE MEETING YOU, SIR.
SAME HERE.

BOBBY!
UH-OH! IT'S MY MOM.
SHE... UH...
DO YOU REALIZE HOW LATE IT IS?!!
SHE DOESN'T REALLY...
...GET...
...THE SUPERHERO LIFESTYLE.
I SWEAR, I DID NOT NOT RAISE YOU TO GO RACING AROUND IN YOUR SKIVIES...
...PLAYING... UMM... OKAY, LET ME SEE... LOTS OF MUD... SO, UHH...
...I'M GUESSING BOG MONSTER.
ACTUALLY, IT WAS A ROWSING GAME OF MIDDLE-AGED DAY-SPA PATRON.
BUT YOU WERE CLOSE.
SIGH
Just... GET in the CAR, okay?
ALL of You.

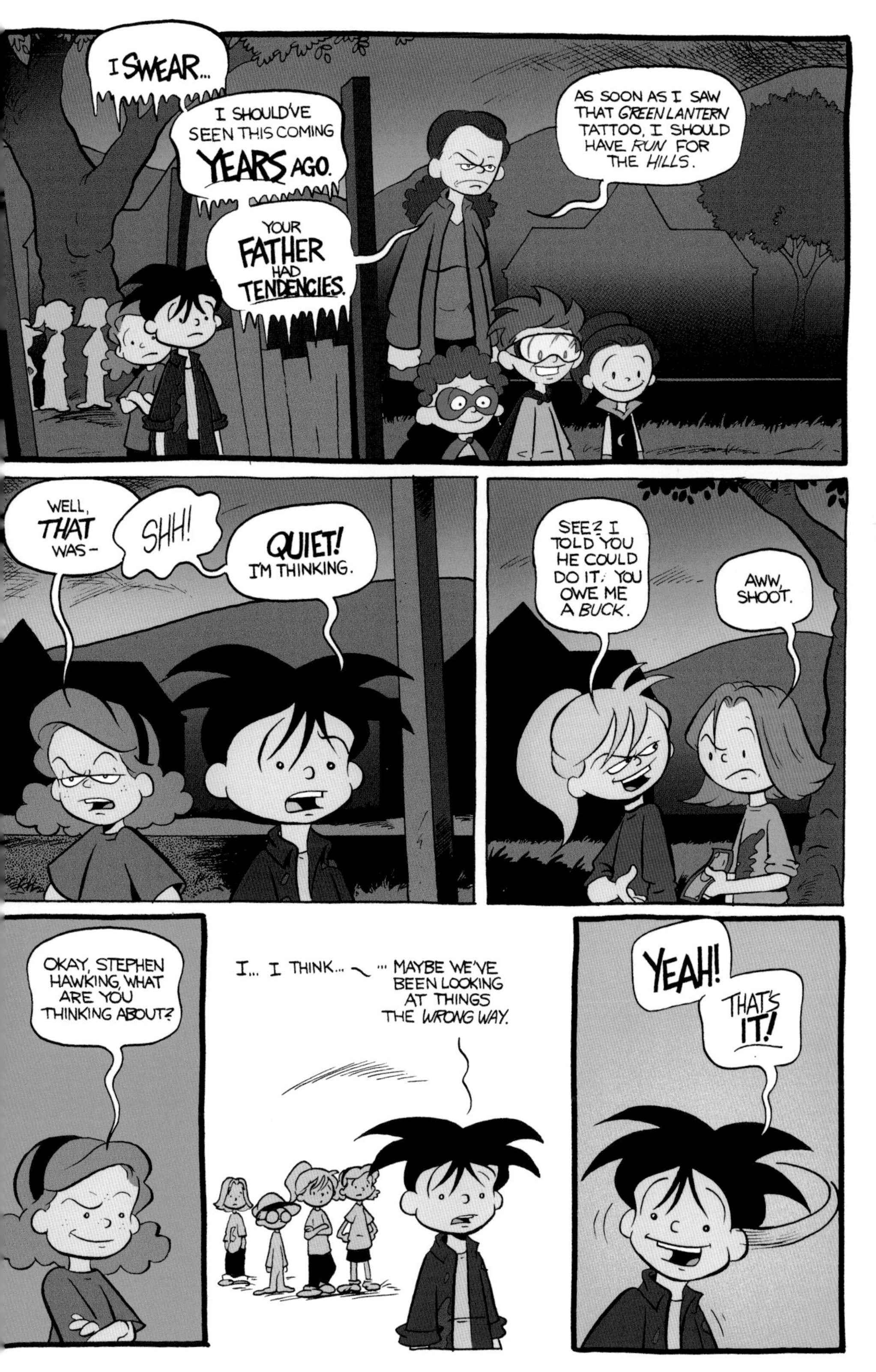
I SWEAR...
I SHOULD'VE SEEN THIS COMING YEARS AGO.
YOUR FATHER HAD TENDENCIES.
AS SOON AS I SAW THAT GREEN LANTERN TATTOO, I SHOULD HAVE RUN FOR THE HILLS.
WELL, THAT WAS-
SHH!
QUIET! I'M THINKING.
SEE? I TOLD YOU HE COULD DO IT. YOU OWE ME A BUCK.
AWW, SHOOT.
OKAY, STEPHEN HAWKING, WHAT ARE YOU THINKING ABOUT?
I... I THINK...
... MAYBE WE'VE BEEN LOOKING AT THINGS THE WRONG WAY.
YEAH!
THAT'S IT!

SEE, ALL THIS TIME, WE'VE BEEN THINKING THAT WE WERE NERDS!
BUT NOW, I DON'T THINK THAT'S TRUE!
WE... WE...
...WE MUST BE GEEKS!
AND GEEKS...
...ARE TOTALLY IN!
IT ALL MAKES SENSE!
DON'T YOU THINK?
Don't you?
UH, YEAH!
SURE. ABSOLUTELY!
SIGH IF YOU SAY SO.
YEAH!
RIGHT!

MAYBE THINGS ARE TURNING AROUND!
I MEAN, HECK, EVEN THE *CLUBHOUSE* IS COMING TOGETHER!
CRASH!
YOU REALLY SHOULD HAVE SEEN THAT COMING.

SO WE WERE ALL LYING AROUND ON THESE RAFTS, JUST FLOATING IN THIS BIG BEAUTIFUL SWIMMING POOL.
IT WAS REAL PEACEFUL AND QUIET, AND EVERYONE WAS HAVING A GOOD TIME.
I CLOSED MY EYES, AND ALL OF A SUDDEN, I COULD FEEL MY RAFT STARTING TO MOVE FAST, LIKE IT WAS SLIIIIIIIIIIIIIIIIIIIIIIDING DOWNHILL.
WHEN I OPENED MY EYES AGAIN, I WAS IN THE OCEAN.
AND I WAS ALONE.

The next thing I knew
I was alone for
hours (or DAYS, who
knows) and I started
crying.

And somehow, I realized
that my tears were
making the ocean, which
doesn't make any sense
because the ocean was
already there, y'know?
But hey, it was a dream.

Anyway... suddenly, it was night, and the water was really calm, and there were, like, a million stars in the sky.
And the water got so clear and so calm that it reflected the stars, like a mirror.
And pretty soon I couldn't tell what was water and what was sky.
And I had the feeling that this happened to everyone and this was just my turn.

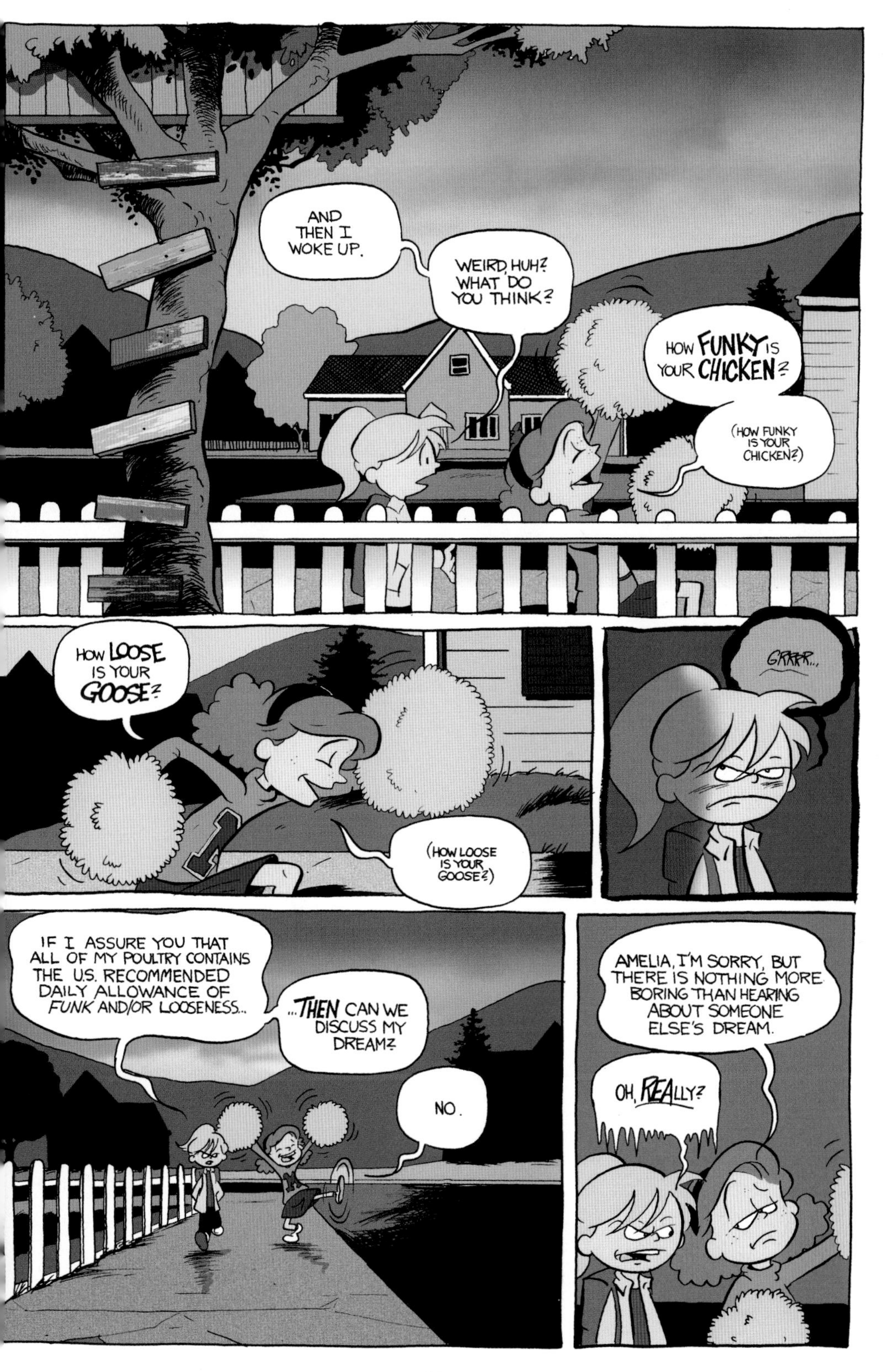
AND THEN I WOKE UP.
WEIRD, HUH? WHAT DO YOU THINK?
HOW FUNKY IS YOUR CHICKEN?
(HOW FUNKY IS YOUR CHICKEN?)
HOW LOOSE IS YOUR GOOSE?
(HOW LOOSE IS YOUR GOOSE?)
GRRRR...
IF I ASSURE YOU THAT ALL OF MY POULTRY CONTAINS THE U.S. RECOMMENDED DAILY ALLOWANCE OF FUNK AND/OR LOOSENESS...
...THEN CAN WE DISCUSS MY DREAM?
NO.
AMELIA, I'M SORRY, BUT THERE IS NOTHING MORE BORING THAN HEARING ABOUT SOMEONE ELSE'S DREAM.
OH, REALLY?

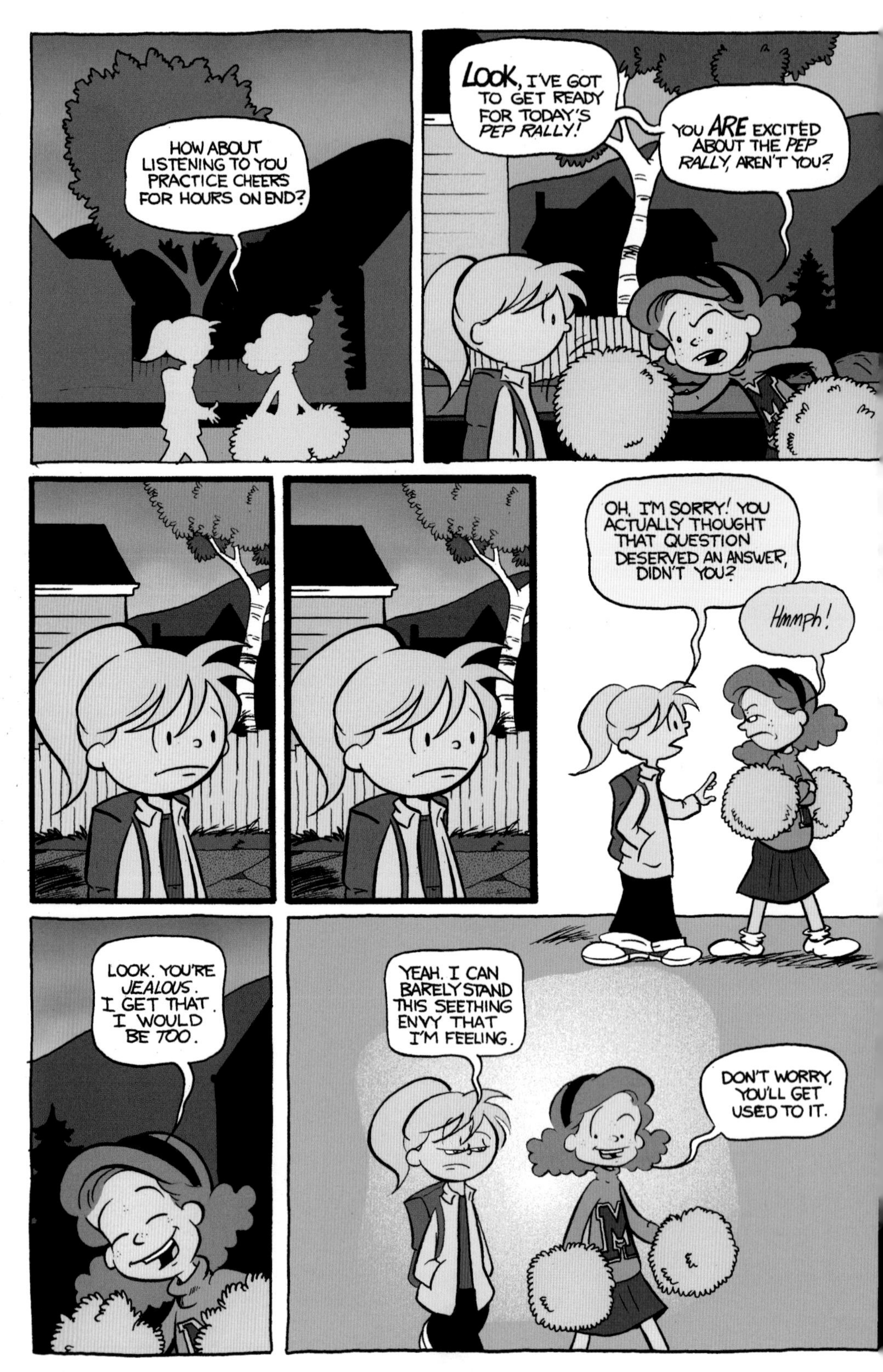
HOW ABOUT LISTENING TO YOU PRACTICE CHEERS FOR HOURS ON END?
LOOK, I'VE GOT TO GET READY FOR TODAY'S PEP RALLY!
YOU ARE EXCITED ABOUT THE PEP RALLY, AREN'T YOU?
OH, I'M SORRY! YOU ACTUALLY THOUGHT THAT QUESTION DESERVED AN ANSWER, DIDN'T YOU?
Hmmph!
LOOK. YOU'RE JEALOUS. I GET THAT. I WOULD BE TOO.
YEAH. I CAN BARELY STAND THIS SEETHING ENVY THAT I'M FEELING.
DON'T WORRY, YOU'LL GET USED TO IT.

AND BEFORE YOU KNOW IT, YOU'LL BE INFUSED WITH SCHOOL SPIRIT.

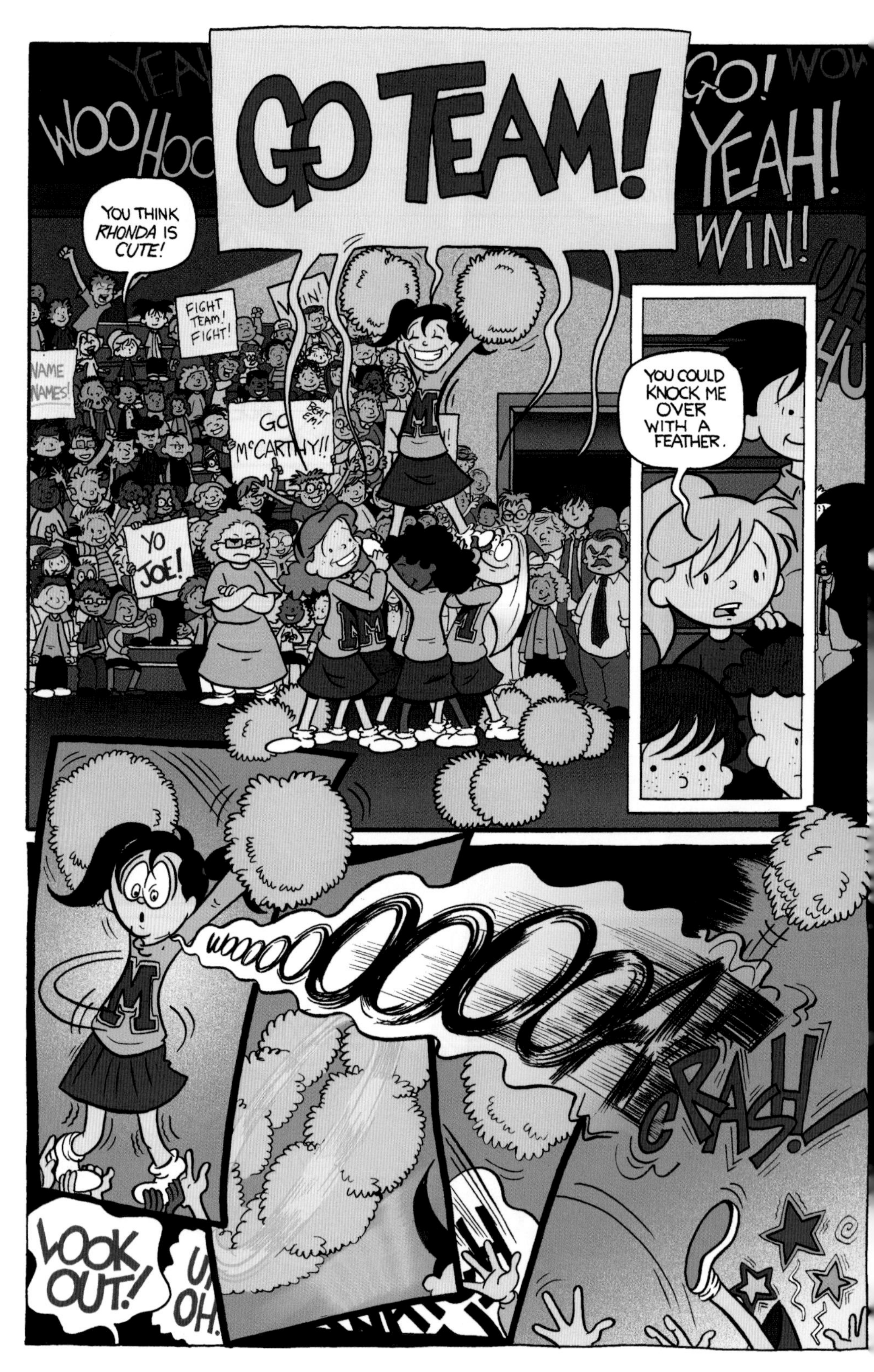

YEAH!
WOO HOO
GO TEAM!
GO!
WOW
YEAH!
WIN!
YOU THINK RHONDA IS CUTE!
FIGHT TEAM! FIGHT!
NAME NAMES!
GO McCARTHY!!
BEAT 'EM!
YO JOE!
YOU COULD KNOCK ME OVER WITH A FEATHER.
WOOOOOOOOOAH!
CRASH!
LOOK OUT!
UH OH.

OOOOOOOOOOOOOOOOo

PUFF PUFF
MAKE WAY! MAKE WAY!
ARE YOU OKAY?!
PUFF
OKAY? I... I THINK...
...I THINK I...
I THINK I'M GONNA SUE SOMEONE! I'M GONNA SUE THE SCHOOL, AND THE FLOOR WAX MANUFACTURER, AND... AND... MY STEPDAD, (WHY NOT?) AND THE OTHER CHEERLEADERS
SHE...UH...SHE DIDN'T SAY PRINCIPAL DID SHE?
UH, NO. NO, I DON'T THINK SO.
GOOD NEWS!
SHE'S GOING TO BE OKAY!

YEAH, SHE'LL BE ALL RIGHT, BUT SHE BUSTED HER KNEE PRETTY BAD.
OUCH.
I KNOW! AND SHE'S GONNA MISS ALL OF SPRING SOCCER.
THAT STINKS! WHAT ARE YOU GUYS GONNA DO?
OH, IT'S OKAY! WE'LL JUST CALL UP THE ALTERNATE.
RIGHT. THAT MAKES SENSE.
YEAH.
>giggle<
SO...
CONGRATULATIONS!
THANKS. I-
WAIT.
WHAT?!

LOVE!
LIFE
FRIENDSHIP
TRUTH
CANDY MAKING 101
BEAUTY

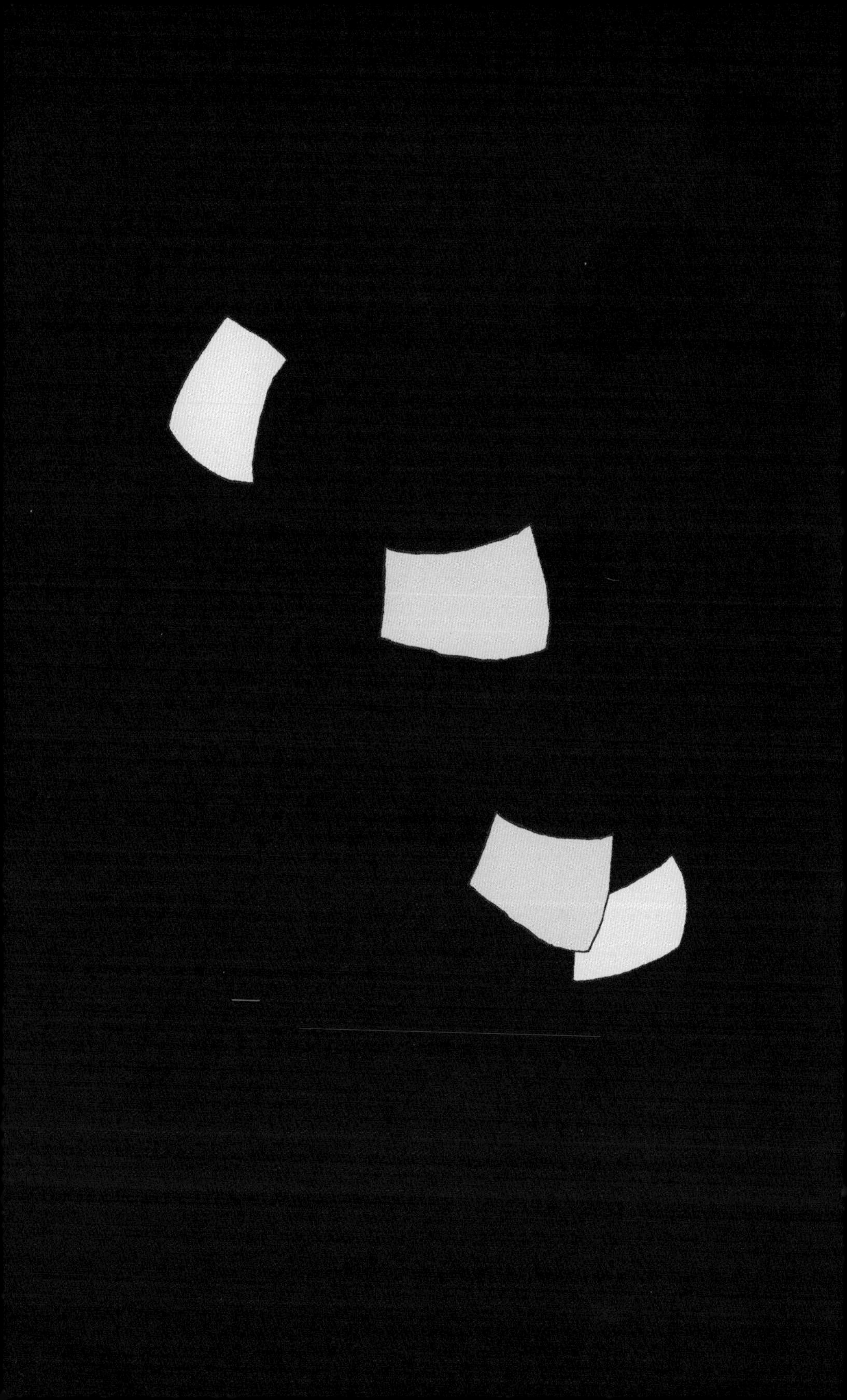

How's the new school?
Have you made some friends?

Oh, you know me....
I always make friends.

That's true. Even when we were in
Alaska, with no other kids on base!

I'm still the only kid I know who was
friends with a stuffed moose!

Anyway, There are a bunch of
kids at my school who are cool.

So, what have you been
doing for fun?

OH, Y'KNOW, CREATE SUPERHERO IDENTITIES, RELIGIOUSLY FOLLOW CULTLIKE SELF-HELP BOOKS....
...HANG OUT WITH THE OCCASIONAL FADED ROCK STAR...
...THE USUAL.
REALLY?
WOW, ME TOO!
HA HA HA HA HA HA
ARMY
I LOVE YOU.
GOOD NIGHT.
GOOD MORNING.
I LOVE YOU TOO.

Everything to Everyone
ONE OF THE GREAT JOYS OF HAVING MY DAD AROUND...
...(OTHER THAN, Y'KNOW, HAVING HIM AROUND)...
...WAS GETTING TO SHOW HIM THE TOWN.

NOW, I'M PRETTY SURE MY DAD LEFT MANHATTAN, LIKE, FOUR TIMES IN THE PAST TEN YEARS.
SO, ARE THERE ANY YANKEES FANS AROUND HERE?
ACTUALLY, IT'S MOSTLY PIRATES FANS.
WHICH IS ALMOST THE SAME AS NOT LIKING BASEBALL AT ALL.
WELL, THERE'S SOMETHING TO BE SAID FOR LOYALTY.
^ GUESS THE BIG EXCITEMENT IS THAT THIS IS THE TOWN'S BICENTENNIAL.
THERE'S GONNA BE LIKE A BLOCK PARTY OR SOMETHING IN A FEW WEEKS.
BE STILL MY TREMBLNG HEART.
SO, THIS WAS BOUND TO BE A BIT OF AN ADJUSTMENT.

AND OVER THERE IS THE OL' FIVE-AND-DIME STORE.
THERE'S AN OLD FIVE-AND-DIME STORE, REALLY?
HARRY'S 5 AND
1926
WELL, YOU DIDN'T EXPECT A NEW FIVE-AND-DIME, DID YOU?
GOOD POINT.
SIGH AND DOWN THERE IS THE SCHOOL.
GREAT!
SO, SHOW ME THE LOCAL HOUSE O' LEARNIN'.
SORRY, I TRY NOT TO GET WITHIN A HUNDRED YARDS OF THE SCHOOL ON A SATURDAY.
IT'S AGAINST MY BELIEFS.
?
YOUR BELIEFS?
YEAH, MY BELIEF THAT THE LESS TIME I SPEND NEAR THE SCHOOL, THE LESS LIKELY I AM TO DISMANTLE IT WITH MY TEETH.
WELL, NEVER LET IT BE SAID THAT I STOOD BETWEEN A WOMAN AND HER FAITH.

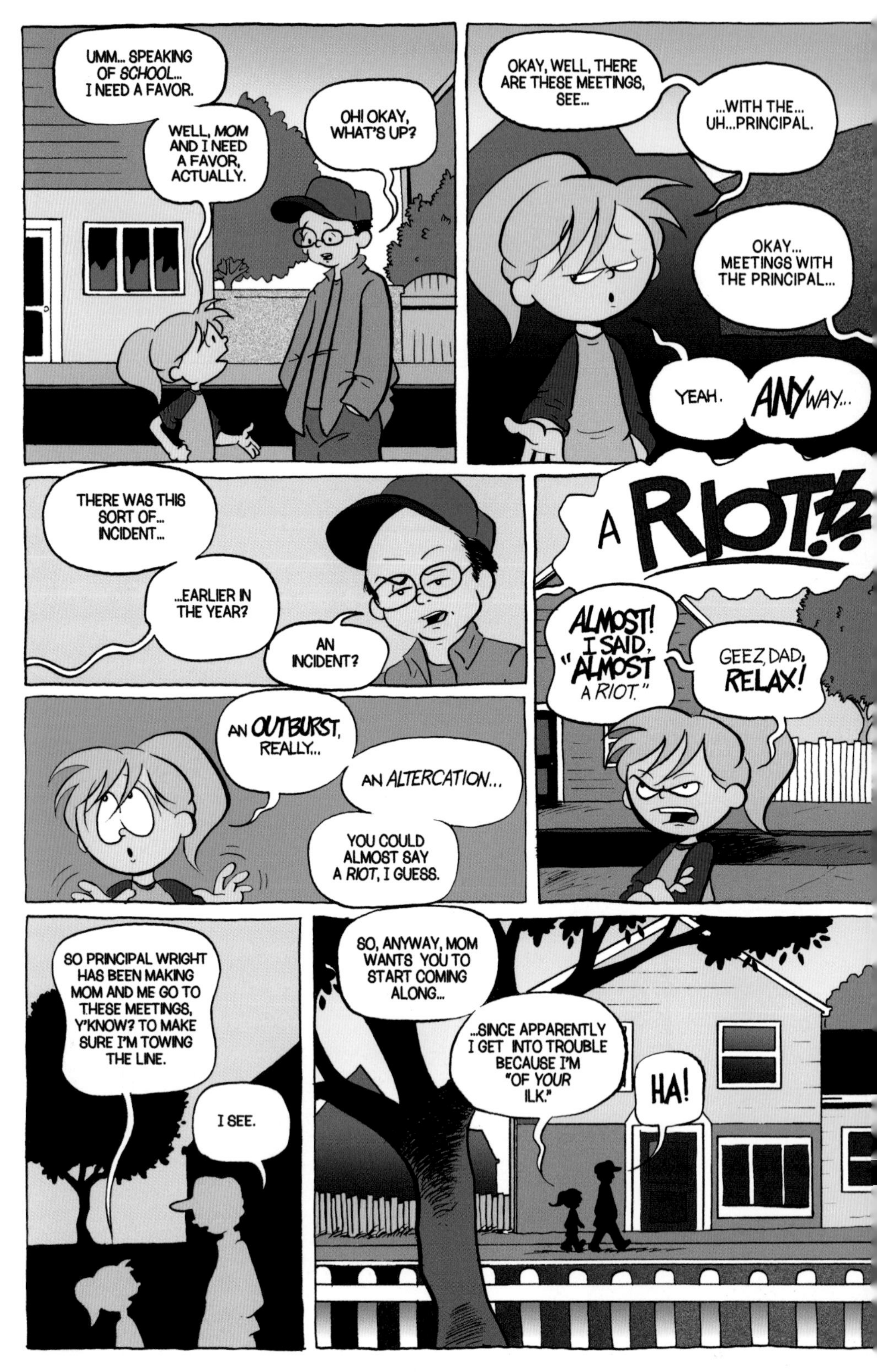
UMM... SPEAKING OF SCHOOL... I NEED A FAVOR.
WELL, MOM AND I NEED A FAVOR, ACTUALLY.
OH! OKAY, WHAT'S UP?
OKAY, WELL, THERE ARE THESE MEETINGS, SEE...
...WITH THE... UH...PRINCIPAL.
OKAY... MEETINGS WITH THE PRINCIPAL...
YEAH.
ANYWAY...
THERE WAS THIS SORT OF... INCIDENT...
...EARLIER IN THE YEAR?
AN INCIDENT?
A RIOT?!
AN OUTBURST, REALLY...
AN ALTERCATION...
YOU COULD ALMOST SAY A RIOT, I GUESS.
ALMOST! I SAID, "ALMOST A RIOT."
GEEZ, DAD, RELAX!
SO PRINCIPAL WRIGHT HAS BEEN MAKING MOM AND ME GO TO THESE MEETINGS, Y'KNOW? TO MAKE SURE I'M TOWING THE LINE.
I SEE.
SO, ANYWAY, MOM WANTS YOU TO START COMING ALONG...
...SINCE APPARENTLY I GET INTO TROUBLE BECAUSE I'M "OF YOUR ILK."
HA!

SO WHEN IS THE NEXT ONE?
TOMORROW AFTER SCHOOL.
OKAY, I'LL BE THERE.
WELL, THIS IS JOAN'S STREET.
CAN YOU FIND YOUR WAY BACK?
I THINK SO.
IF NOT, I'LL JUST GRAB A CAB.
SIGH
AND HE WAS NEVER SEEN AGAIN.
DON'T BE SUCH A SMART MOUTH.
TOO LATE.

I LOVE JOAN DRISCOLL.
SHE'S FUN AND CRAZY AND TOUGH AND SUPER, *SUPER* WEIRD.
THAT WAS...
UH!
MAY!
ZING!
BOUNCE BOUNCE
BOUNCE BOUNCE
ARMY
BWANG!
TANNER ROCKS SO HARD! SHE WAS ALL LIKE...
OH YEAH!
OH BABY YEAH! YEAH! YEAH!
I FEEL LIKE I COULD TALK TO HER ABOUT *ANYTHING.*
WELL, ALMOST ANYTHING.
AND HER GUITAR WAS ALL...
BWANG! BWANG! BWANG!
AND THEN SHE'S LIKE...
GOOD NIGHT!
HER DAD'S IN THE ARMY. A FEW MONTHS AGO, HE WAS SENT AWAY...TO FIGHT, I GUESS.
JOAN DOESN'T TALK ABOUT IT MUCH, WHICH IS OKAY, I GUESS.
IF SHE DID, I WOULDN'T KNOW WHAT TO SAY.

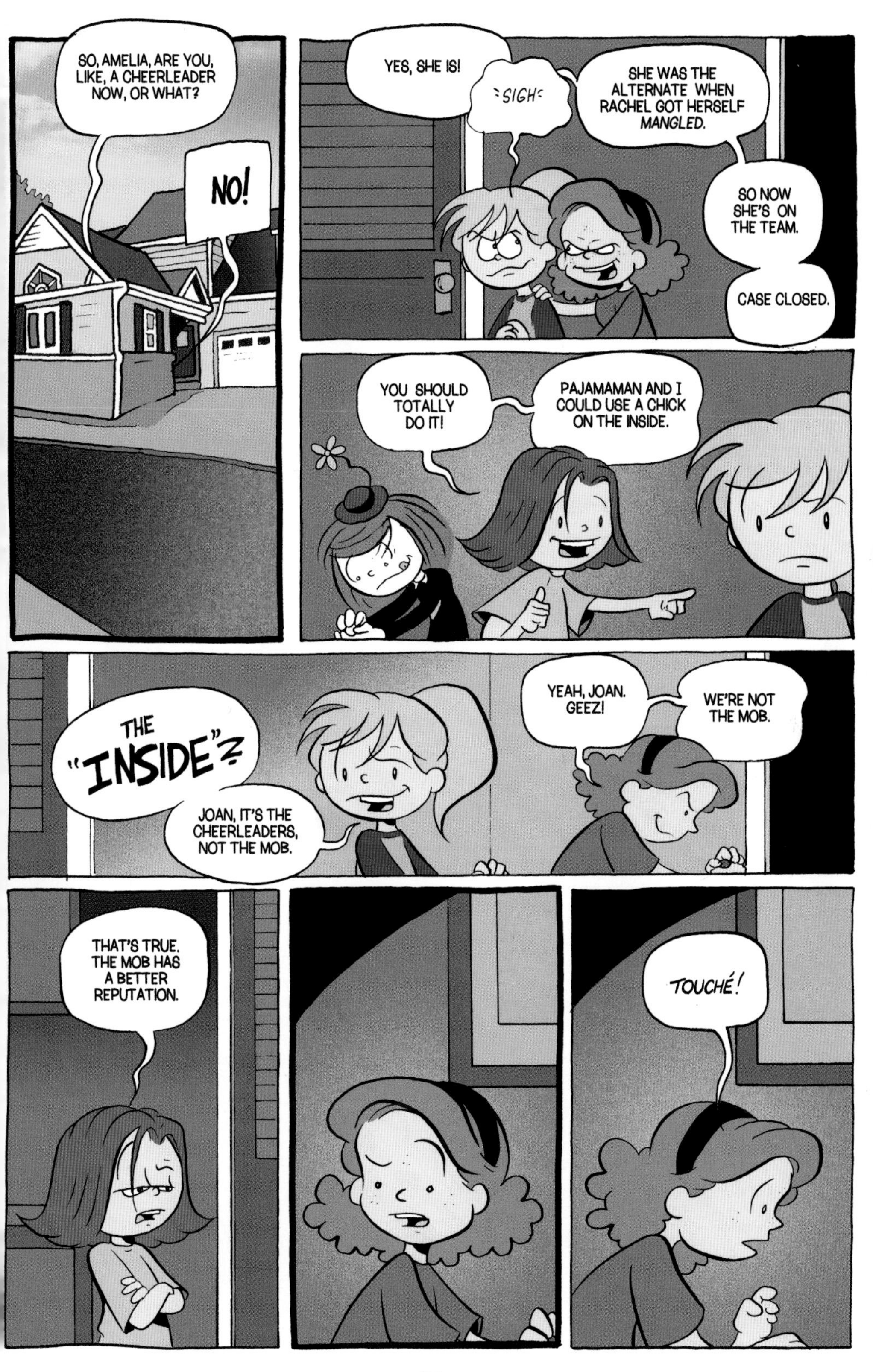
SO, AMELIA, ARE YOU, LIKE, A CHEERLEADER NOW, OR WHAT?
NO!
YES, SHE IS!
SIGH
SHE WAS THE ALTERNATE WHEN RACHEL GOT HERSELF *MANGLED.*
SO NOW SHE'S ON THE TEAM.
CASE CLOSED.
YOU SHOULD TOTALLY DO IT!
PAJAMAMAN AND I COULD USE A CHICK ON THE INSIDE.
THE "INSIDE"?
JOAN, IT'S THE CHEERLEADERS, NOT THE MOB.
YEAH, JOAN. GEEZ!
WE'RE NOT THE MOB.
THAT'S TRUE. THE MOB HAS A BETTER REPUTATION.
TOUCHÉ!

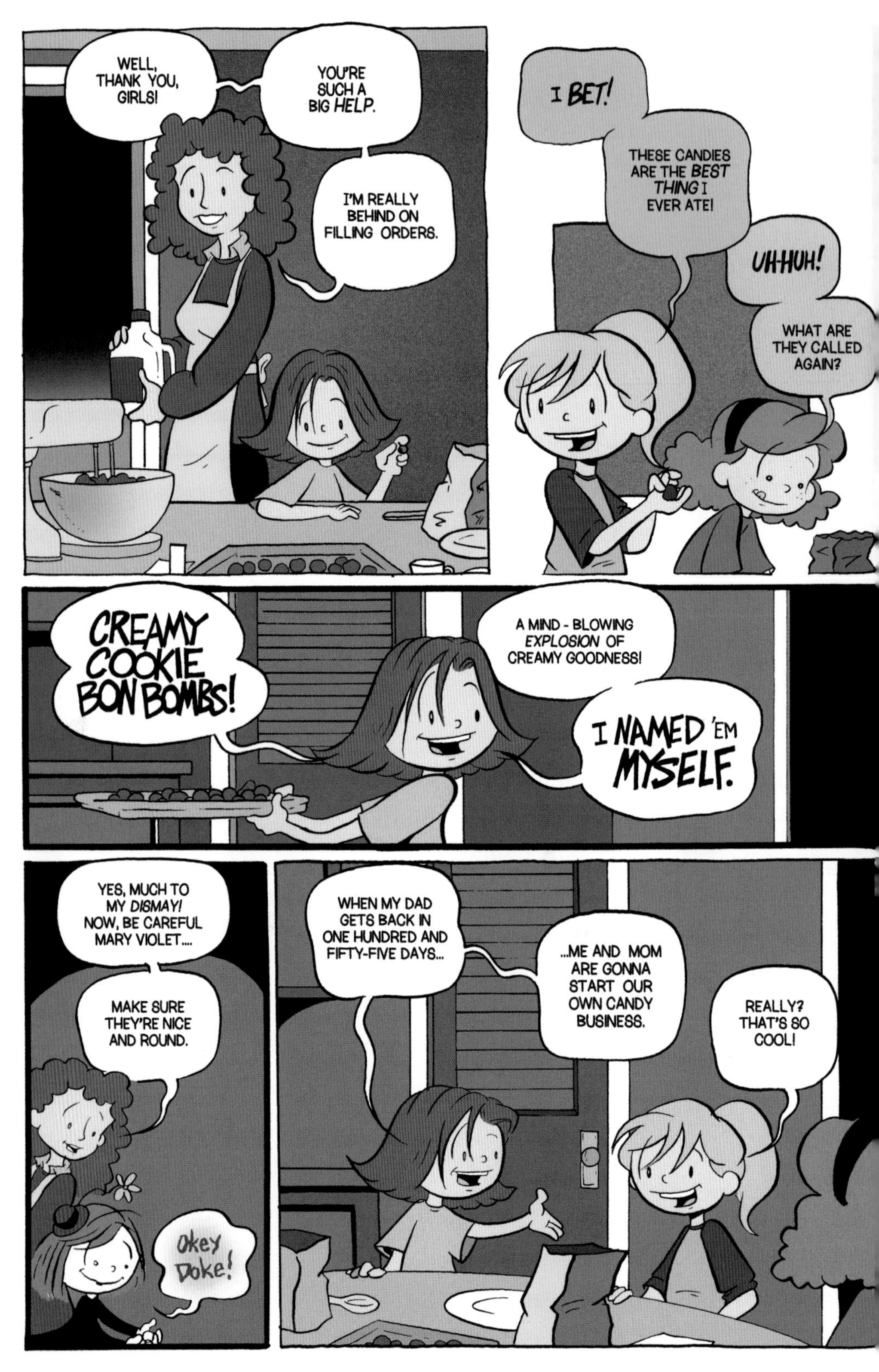
WELL, THANK YOU, GIRLS!
YOU'RE SUCH A BIG *HELP*.
I'M REALLY BEHIND ON FILLING ORDERS.
I *BET!*
THESE CANDIES ARE THE *BEST THING* I EVER ATE!
UH-HUH!
WHAT ARE THEY CALLED AGAIN?
CREAMY COOKIE BON BOMBS!
A MIND - BLOWING *EXPLOSION* OF CREAMY GOODNESS!
I NAMED 'EM MYSELF.
YES, MUCH TO MY *DISMAY!* NOW, BE CAREFUL MARY VIOLET....
MAKE SURE THEY'RE NICE AND ROUND.
Okey Doke!
WHEN MY DAD GETS BACK IN ONE HUNDRED AND FIFTY-FIVE DAYS...
...ME AND MOM ARE GONNA START OUR OWN CANDY BUSINESS.
REALLY? THAT'S SO COOL!

NOW, JOAN, DON'T GET AHEAD OF YOURSELF.
THAT'S MONTHS AWAY, AND WE HAVEN'T EVEN MENTIONED IT TO YOUR FATHER.
SIGH
I KNOW I KNOW...
I'M JUST DREAMING A LITTLE!
OKAY, THEN.
DON'T LET HER FOOL YOU.
THESE SUCKERS ARE BUYING ME A NEW LAPTOP.
SWEET!
GAH!
These things are Sticky!
LET'S SEE...
...TWO TINS...
...A LARGE BAG...
...AND TWO SMALL BOXES.
OKAY!
SOUNDS LIKE IT'S TIME FOR A DELIVERY RUN.

THE DELIVERY SYSTEM NEEDS SOME WORK..
...BUT WHAT THE HECK...
...THESE GUYS ARE CHEAP.
ARE YOU TWO READY?
WELL, IT'S ABOUT TIME!
YOU THINK WE HAVE NOTHING ELSE TO DO?
ACTUALLY, WE *KNOW* YOU HAVE NOTHING BETTER TO DO.
OKAY, OKAY, GUYS. HERE'S THE LATEST BATCH...
...AND HERE'RE THE ADDRESSES.
AND CAN YOU *TRY* NOT TO EAT ANY OF THE ORDERS THIS TIME?!
SPOILSPORT!
the CANDY CAR
HEY, RHONDA, DO YOU WANNA COME FOR THE RIDE?
NO THANKS.
MAYBE NEXT TIME.
OH!
OKAY... UH...
...RIGHT THEN...
...NEXT TIME!

ARE YOU SURE THIS PIECE OF JUNK IS ACTUALLY ROAD-WORTHY?
WHAT?! YOU INSULT ME??
JOAN...
...THIS...
...IS THE AMAZING MOBILE!
CANDY MOBILE!
THIS IS WHAT CARRIED US INTO OUR EPIC BATTLE AGAINST THE STEVES.
SHE MADE THE DONUT RUN IN LESS THAN TWELVE PARSECS.
AND SURE, SHE MAY NOT HAVE BRAKES, OR AN EFFECTIVE STEERING MECHANISM, BUT SHE'S GOT WHAT COUNTS...
...HEART!
AND THAT MEANS?
WE SHOULD BE OKAY IF ALL OF THE ADDRESSES ARE STRAIGHT DOWN A LIGHTLY TRAVELED HILL.
OKAY, LET'S SEE.
DUKE, MAPLE, MARKET, WILLOW, CHATHAM.
HEY, I THINK THESE ARE ALL—
WE'RE OFF!
CANDY MOBILE!

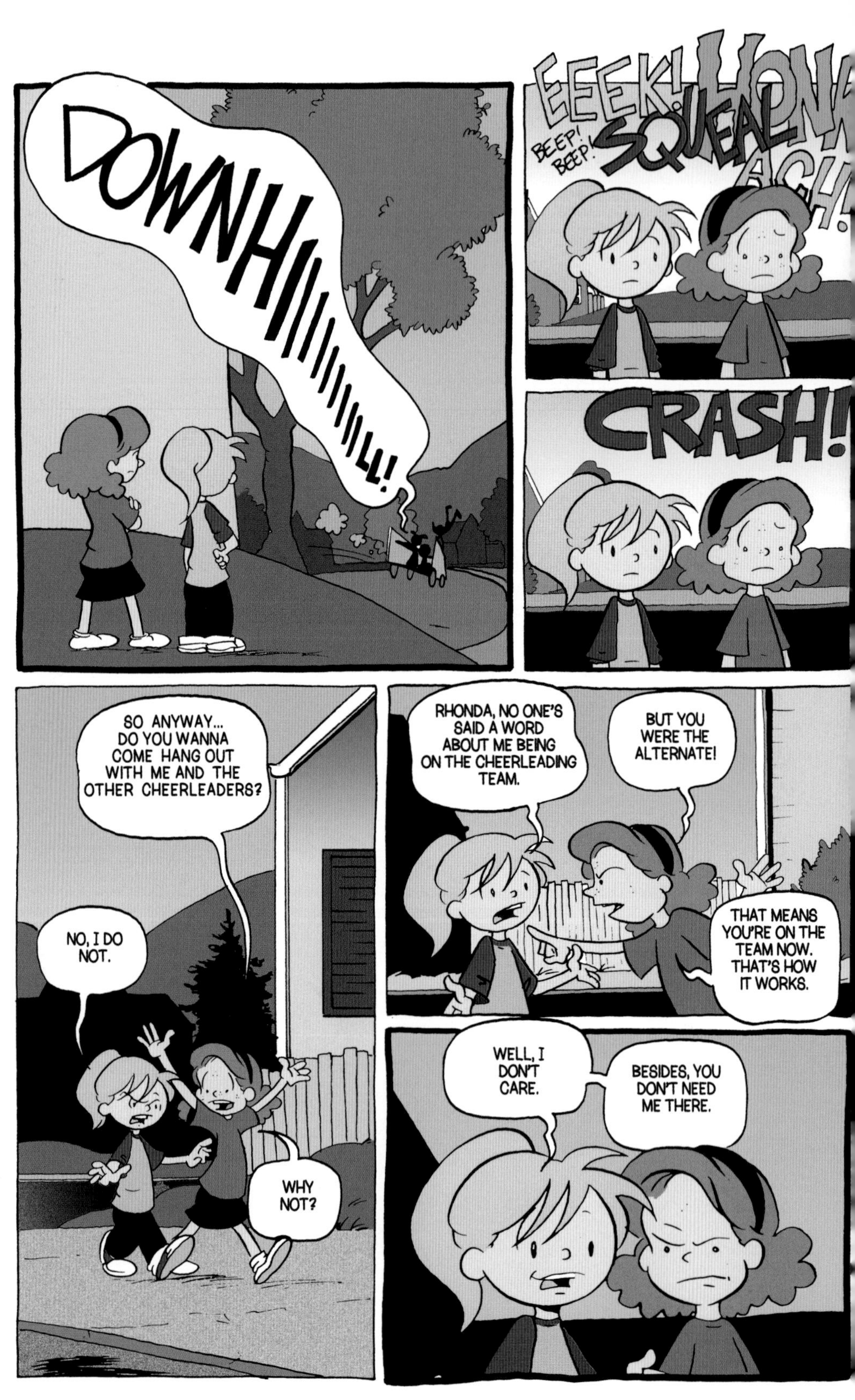
DOWNHIIIIIIIIIIILL!
EEEK!
HONK
BEEP! BEEP!
SQUEAL
ACH!
CRASH!
SO ANYWAY... DO YOU WANNA COME HANG OUT WITH ME AND THE OTHER CHEERLEADERS?
NO, I DO NOT.
WHY NOT?
RHONDA, NO ONE'S SAID A WORD ABOUT ME BEING ON THE CHEERLEADING TEAM.
BUT YOU WERE THE ALTERNATE!
THAT MEANS YOU'RE ON THE TEAM NOW. THAT'S HOW IT WORKS.
WELL, I DON'T CARE.
BESIDES, YOU DON'T NEED ME THERE.

OF COURSE, I SHOULD HAVE REMEMBERED THAT RHONDA WAS NEVER GOOD AT TAKING A HINT!

NOW SURE, HAVING RHONDA BEG FOR MY HELP WAS PRETTY SATISFYING.
BUT AFTER A WHILE EVEN THAT BECAME ANNOYING
I MEAN, IT GOT PRETTY PATHETIC.
C'MON! I'LL BE YOUR BEST FRIEND.
NO!
I'LL FEED YOUR GOLDFISH EVERY DAY FOR A YEAR!
I DON'T HAVE A FISH!
OKAY, I WILL BUY YOU A FISH, THEN I'LL FEED IT!
JUST SHUT UP!
HOW ABOUT IF I *NEVER* MENTION HOW YOUR HEAD IS TOO BIG FOR YOUR NECK AGAIN!
RHONDA!
THE WAY I SAW IT, I GAVE UP THE CHANCE TO BE A CHEERLEADER SO RHONDA COULD HAVE IT.
I'D PUT IT BEHIND ME! I'D MOVED ON.
BUT THEN I FIGURED...

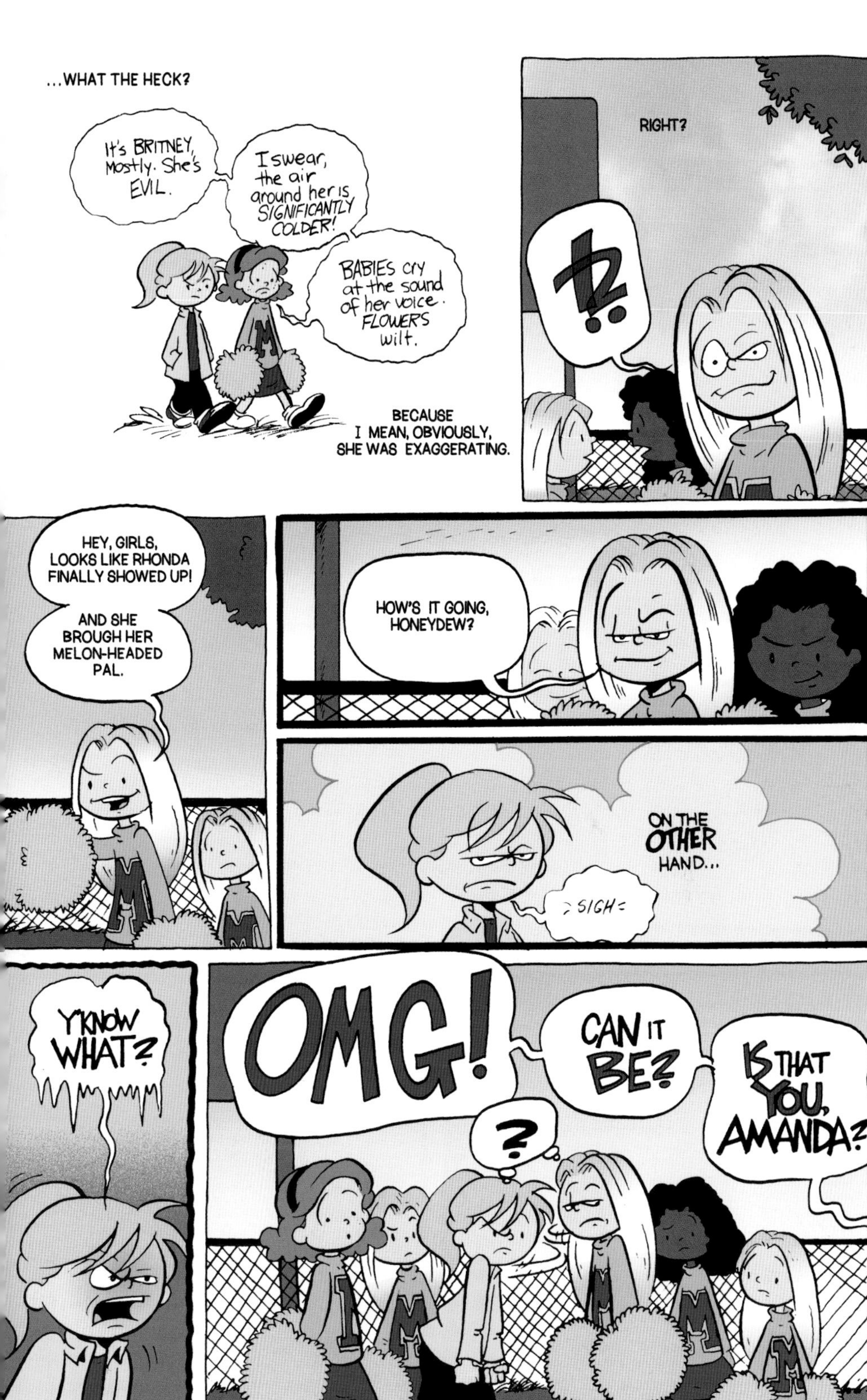
...WHAT THE HECK?
It's BRITNEY, Mostly. She's EVIL.
I swear, the air around her is SIGNIFICANTLY COLDER!
BABIES cry at the sound of her voice. FLOWERS wilt.
BECAUSE I MEAN, OBVIOUSLY, SHE WAS EXAGGERATING.
RIGHT?
!?
HEY, GIRLS, LOOKS LIKE RHONDA FINALLY SHOWED UP!
AND SHE BROUGH HER MELON-HEADED PAL.
HOW'S IT GOING, HONEYDEW?
ON THE OTHER HAND...
SIGH
Y'KNOW WHAT?
OMG!
CAN IT BE?
IS THAT YOU, AMANDA?
?

UH...
...AMELIA, ACTUALLY.
RIGHT, OF COURSE! SO GOOD TO SEE YOU!
I HAD NEVER, IN MY ENTIRE LIFE, HAD AN ADULT ASSOCIATED WITH THIS SCHOOL SO EXCITED TO SEE ME.
HOW ARE YOU?
FRANKLY, IT WAS TERRIFYING!
UHH...
...OKAY...
I GUESS.
SUPER!
GIRLS, I WANT YOU ALL TO WELCOME... AMELIA...OUR NEWEST CHEERLEADER.
!
TERRIFIC!
CLAP
CLAP
CLAP

WAIT A MINUTE, COACH.
WE'VE BEEN WORKING HARD FOR A LONG TIME, AND WE'VE GOTTEN BETTER SINCE TRYOUTS.
HOW DO WE KNOW AMELIA IS GOOD ENOUGH? SHE SHOULD HAVE TO TRY OUT AGAIN.
BRITNEY, I REALLY DON'T THINK THAT'S NECESSARY.
NO!
IT'S OKAY...
...IF BRITNEY WANTS TO SEE IT...
...I'D BE HAPPY TO SHOW HER WHAT I CAN DO.
THEN DO IT.
I WILL!
I'M WAITING.
THEN HERE IT IS.

AND SO
(FIVE MINUTES LATER...)
THAT WAS...
...INCREDIBLE!
THE FLIPS!
THE HANDSTANDS!
THE CART-WHEELS!
HAVE YOU BEEN PRACTICING?
UHH...
HIT 'EM HIGH!
HIT 'EM LOW!
NOPE.
BEGINNER'S LUCK, I GUESS!

SO, PRACTICE IS MONDAYS, WEDNESDAYS, AND FRIDAYS.
AND WE'LL GET YOU A UNIFORM ONCE WE CAN PRY IT AWAY FROM RACHEL.
I HEAR SHE STILL SLEEPS IN IT.
OKAY.
MONDAYS, WEDNESDAYS, AND FRIDAYS.
GOT IT!
OH! EXCEPT SOMETIMES I HAVE TO GO TO A MEETING ON MONDAAAAACK!
AWSHOOTIGOTTAGO!!
PTWIIIIIIING!!
WOW.
SHE MUST REALLY BE EXCITED TO TELL PEOPLE SHE MADE THE TEAM.

OH, SHOOT!
OH, SHOOT!
OH, SHOOT!
OH, SHOOT!
OH, SHOOT!
I'M HERE!

I'M-
GLP
UHH...
HI... UHH... E-EVERYONE.
SKREEEEET
I'M LATE! I'M LATE! I KNOW!
AND I'M SURE YOU'RE WONDERING WHAT HAPPENED.
WELL, FUNNY YOU SHOULD ASK—
AMELIA!
NOW IS NOT THE TIME FOR "FUNNY STORIES."
NOW IS THE TIME FOR YOU TO SIT AND LISTEN.
UNDERSTAND?
YEAH.
I UNDERSTAND.

YES, THE GRADES ARE MUCH BETTER
BEHAVIOR, HOWEVER... WELL, I'VE BEEN WATCHING HER MYSELF LATELY...
...AND, WELL, I MEAN, HER LANGUAGE ALONE IS JUST...
...WELL, IT'S SHOCKING.
AND KEEP IN MIND, THIS IS JUST WHAT I OVERHEARD LAST WEEK!
"DOOFUS."
"LOUSY."
"STUPID."
"SCHMUCK."
"CRAPPY." (I MEAN, REALLY...)
IS THAT APPROPRIATE?
AND FOR A YOUNG LADY, TOO!

THESE THINGS, THE LANGUAGE, THE TARDINESS...
...THE CONSTANT TESTING OF BOUNDARIES.
THEY'RE ALL PART OF A DESPERATE CRY FOR ATTENTION.
PFFT! YOU
I'LL YOU
Z!
MUMBLING UNDER YOUR BREATH ISN'T GOING TO HELP YOUR CAUSE.
WHAT WILL IS LEARNING TO STRAIGHTEN UP AND FLY RIGHT.
DO YOU UNDERSTAND?
YEAH....
I GET IT.
SIGH
GROWN-UPS ARE THE WORST.

WELL...
MOST GROWN-UPS...
THIS IS ABSOLUTELY DELICIOUS!
MARY, THANK YOU SO MUCH FOR HAVING ME OVER.
WE BACHELORS DON'T OFTEN GET A NICE HOME-COOKED MEAL.
HOME-COOKED?
I THOUGHT YOU OPENED THIS FROM SIMPLY CHICK—
OW!
QUIT KICKING!
SO!
HAVE YOU HEARD FROM OUR GIRL LATELY?

WELL, WE E-MAIL BACK AND FORTH, BUT SHE IS INCREDIBLY BUSY.
I THINK IT'S A LOT OF PRESSURE FOR HER.
THE WHOLE TOUR, I MEAN.
WELL, I SUPPOSE YOU'RE EXTREMELY BUSY YOURSELF.
KEEPING TRACK OF A ROOM FULL OF FIFTH GRADERS.
ABSOLUTELY.
TEACHING IS AN INCREDIBLY DEMANDING PROFESSION.
I CAN IMAGINE!
MR. HENDERSON? CAN I ASK YOU SOMETHING?
OF COURSE.
WHY ON EARTH WOULD ANYONE WANT TO BE A TEACHER?
I MEAN, SERIOUSLY...
IF I HAD TO GO TO SCHOOL EVERY DAY FOR THE REST OF MY LIFE...
...I'D GO CATCH A BUS WITH MY FACE.
HA!

WELL, SCHOOL CAN BE A LOT MORE FUN ONCE YOU'RE NOT THE ONE BEING GRADED.
HMM... YEAH, I CAN SEE THAT.
BUT SCHOOL'S NOT ALL I DO, Y'KNOW?
I'M A BIT OF A WRITER AS WELL.
SHORT STORIES MOSTLY.
REALLY! HAVE YOU HAD ANY PUBLISHED?
A FEW.
IT'S BEEN GREAT, ACTUALLY. I'VE GOTTEN A FANTASTIC RESPONSE.
I'M WORKING ON A BOOK RIGHT NOW.
ACTUALLY, I SORT OF FEEL LIKE I'M ALWAYS WORKING ON A BOOK. I'VE KEPT A JOURNAL SINCE I WAS A KID.
IT'S ONE OF THE THINGS TANNER AND I BONDED OVER.
WHAT?
I NEVER KNEW SHE KEPT A DIARY!
WELL, THAT'S TANNER, I GUESS. SHE'S A MYSTERY.

WELL, I GUESS MR. HENDERSON WAS RIGHT ABOUT THAT.
MY AUNT TANNER *IS* A MYSTERY.
LIKE, IT WAS A MYSTERY HOW WE COULD BE SO CLOSE FOR SO LONG, AND NOW SHE DOESN'T EVEN REPLY TO MY E-MAILS.
ANYWAY...
WHAT *WASN'T* MYSTERIOUS WAS MY MOM.
I FIGURED THE WHOLE REASON SHE INVITED MY TEACHER OVER WAS FOR US TO TALK. LIKE, TO BOND, OR WHATEVER
WHICH WAS OKAY, I GUESS.
AT LEAST IT WAS SOMEONE TO TALK TO.
HE JUST HATES ME, Y'KNOW?
THERE'S NOTHING I CAN DO.

WELL, LOOK...IT'S NOT LIKE PRINCIPAL WRIGHT AND I ARE BFFs OR ANYTHING...
...BUT HE *DOES* HAVE A POINT.
BOOM
AMELIA?
AMELIA, I THINK YOU'RE ONE OF THE SMARTEST KIDS IN YOUR CLASS.
BUT THERE'S *SOMETHING* HOLDING YOU BACK.
GO AHEAD.
I'M LISTENING.
SOMETHING YOU'RE *LETTING* HOLD YOU BACK.
THE ONLY THING HOLDING *ME* BACK...
...IS WRIGHT AND HIS TOTAL HATRED OF ME!

AMELIA, THERE WILL BE PLENTY OF TIMES IN LIFE WHEN YOU'LL HAVE TO DEAL WITH A "PRINCIPAL WRIGHT."
BUT WHEN YOU DO...
...TRY LISTENING TO THE BETTER ANGELS OF YOUR NATURE...
...INSTEAD OF Y'KNOW...
GOING ALL "PUNK ROCK"?
EXACTLY.
BUT HEY...
YOU DON'T HAVE TO GO ALL EASY LISTENING EITHER.
AND LISTEN...
I KNOW I'M NOT HER...
BUT IF YOU EVER NEED TO TALK...
THANKS.

HE'S RIGHT YOU KNOW.
YOU SHOULD LISTEN TO ME MORE.
WHAT, MY INNER SUPERHERO?
THE ANGEL OF YOUR BETTER NATURE.

LOVE!
LIFE
FRIENDSHIP
TRUTH
CANDY
MAKING 101
BEAUTY

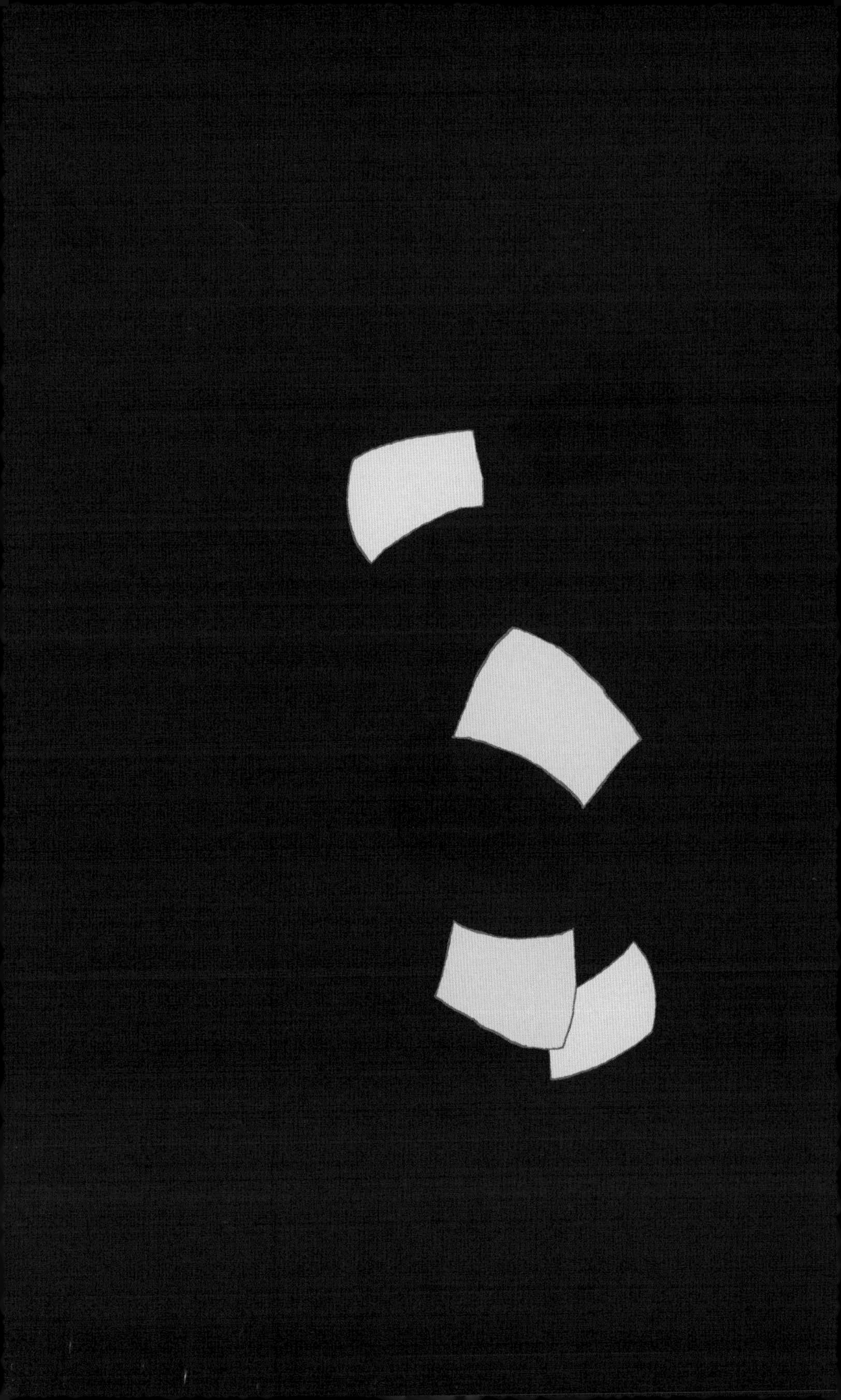

Y'KNOW WHAT I'VE NOTICED? EVERYONE AROUND ME HAS AN OPINION OF ME. AND EVERY ONE IS DIFFERENT.
TO MOM AND DAD, I'LL ALWAYS BE A BABY (FIG. 1).
BUT TO THE Y.I.K.E.S KIDS, I'M LIKE A HERO (FIG. 2).
fig.1
AWW!
fig.2
HOORAY!
P
AND SOMEHOW, MR. HENDERSON THINKS I'M A BRAIN (FIG. 3).
WHILE PRINCIPAL WRIGHT STILL THINKS I'M BAD (FIG. 4).
AND MOST OF MY CLASS JUST THINKS I'M A LOSER (FIG. 5).
WHOA!
fig.3
BOOO!
fig.4
DUH!
DUNCE
2+2=OHIO
fig.5
BUT I CAN'T BE ALL THOSE THINGS AT ONCE...
DUNCE
P

CAN I?
WE USED TO BE FRIENDS
WELL...
WHAT DO YOU THINK?
SHAKE SHAKE
SHAKE
I THINK THAT THE BLUE GOES NICE WITH YOUR COMPLEXION, AND THAT I'M DYING INSIDE.

C'MON, REGGIE, YOU SHOULD BE HAPPY FOR HER.
SHE HAS THE HONOR OF WEARING AN OFFICIAL McCARTHY MAVERICKS CHEERLEADER UNIFORM.
THE ONLY UNIFORM YOU HAVE HAS THE UNDIES ON THE OUTSIDE.
HEY! THAT UNIFORM INSPIRES FEAR IN THE HEARTS OF NINJAS...
...AND STEVES...
...AND MY MINISTER!
LOOK, ALL I'M SAYING IS
Oh, RHONNNDAAAA
WE'RE TAKING YOUR SISTER TO THE MAAAAALL!
WE NEED TO BUY HER SOMETHING EXPENSIVE!!
OKAYEEE I DON'T CARRRE!
OH! I SEE YOUR...
"FRIENDS"...
...ARE HERE.
WELL, TRY NOT TO DO ANYTHING TO HUMILATE THE FAMILEEEEE.
NOOOOOO PROMISES.

THAT'S ONE THING ABOUT RHONDA'S FAMILY... THEY'RE SO MESSED UP. IT MAKES YOU FORGET YOUR OWN PROBLEMS.
WELL...
FOR A MINUTE OR TWO, ANYWAY.
RHONDA, I THINK I'M *FREAKING OUT*!
WHAT? WHY?
IT'S TOO MUCH PRESSURE! I FEEL LIKE I'M MAKING A HUGE MISTAKE!
DON'T WORRY, I'LL BE THERE WITH YOU.
SHAKE
SHAKE
SHAKE
SHAKE
WHAT GOOD WILL THAT DO? YOU'RE AS BAD OFF AS I AM!!
HOW CAN YOU HELP ME?!
WELL, AFTER ALL, I *AM* THE ONE WHO MADE THE SQUAD, RIGHT? I KNOW WHAT I'M DOING.
HUH?
OH! UHH...
RIGHT!
OKAY THEN, STICK WITH ME.

OKAY! IT LOOKS LIKE EVERYONE IS HERE!
GREAT! WE CAN GET STARTED.
BUT FIRST, LET'S HAVE A SPECIAL WELCOME FOR OUR NEWEST MEMBER.
AMANDA McCLOUD!
Heh Heh Heh Heh
GLP
RHONDA, IF I DON'T MAKE IT OUT OF THIS ALIVE, YOU'LL TELL MY FAMILY THAT I LOVED THEM, WON'T YOU?
NO.
THANKS.

OKAY, McBRIDE...
...INITIATION TIME!
INITIATION? WHAT DO—
WHOOA!!!!
FLUMP!
HAHAHAHAHAHAHAHA
HAHAHAHAHAHAHAHA
?
AMELIA!
YOU WERE INCREDIBLE!
REALLY? THANKS!

GREAT JOB, GIRLS!
EXCELLENT PRACTICE!
YOU GIRLS HAVE BEEN WORKING SO HARD, AND IT'S REALLY PAYING OFF.
AND A SPECIAL THANK-YOU AND CONGRATULATIONS TO OUR NEWEST TEAM MEMBER!
CLAP CLAP CLAP CLAP CLAP CLAP CLAP CLAP CLAP
CARE TO SAY A FEW WORDS, AMELIA?
?
OH! UHH... OKAY...
MISS McBRIDE.
REALLY...
?
!
MAY I HAVE A WORD WITH YOU?

SOMEONE WITH YOUR ONGOING DISCIPLINARY PROBLEMS...
...WE COULDN'T POSSIBLY ALLOW ON THE SQUAD.
I MEAN, YOU'D BE REPRESENTING YOUR CLASS...
...THE WHOLE SCHOOL...
...IT'S NOT EVEN REALLY A DECISION...
...IT'S A MATTER OF POLICY....
DO YOU UNDERSTAND?
yes.
GOOD.
AND MAYBE NEXT YEAR, WHEN THINGS ARE...
..."DIFFERENT"...
YEAH.

IF THERE IS A THEME TO MY LIFE, IT'S THIS:
"NOTHING LASTS."
NOT FAMILY.
NOT FRIENDS.
NOT HOMES.
NOT HAPPINESS.
NOT LOVE.
NOT HOPE.
NOT PEACE.
NOT ANYTHING.
(NOT EVEN BEING ON THE STUPID CHEERLEADING SQUAD.)

I WAS SO ANGRY! AND I DIDN'T WANT TO TALK TO MOM
OR DAD, OR REGGIE, OR ANYONE.
I WANTED TO TALK TO TANNER.
BUT THAT DIDN'T MATTER, BECAUSE I DIDN'T HAVE HER ANYMORE.
ALL I HAD WAS THIS:
I'VE KEPT A JOURNAL SINCE I WAS A KID. IT'S ONE OF THE THINGS TANNER AND I BONDED OVER.
IT WASN'T MUCH, BUT LIKE I SAID, IT WAS ALL I HAD.
I FIGURED IF TANNER HAD KEPT A DIARY, MAYBE IT WAS STILL AROUND.
THE FIRST PLACE I CHECKED WAS THE ATTIC OF HER OLD HOUSE...
...BUT EVERYTHING HAD BEEN CLEANED OUT WHEN THEY PUT THE NEW STUDIO IN.
THEN I REMEMBERED ALL THE OLD MEMENTOS FROM TANNER'S CAREER THAT MY MOM HAD KEPT.

I FIGURED IT
WAS WORTH
A SHOT.
Hmmm...
AHA!
TANNER
CLARK

I ROOTED AROUND FOR HOURS, AND ALL I CAME UP WITH...
...WERE TWO NOTEBOOKS...
TANNER CLARK
...FROM, LIKE, TWENTY YEARS APART...
Tanner Clark
...AND AN OLD MAGAZINE INTERVIEW.
PRETTY SLIM PICKINGS, REALLY, BUT I WAS DESPERATE.

I GUESS THERE WAS PROBABLY SOME SMALL PART OF ME THAT THOUGHT IT WAS WRONG TO READ TANNER'S OLD DIARIES AND STUFF...
...BUT TO BE HONEST, THAT PART BARELY PUT UP A FIGHT. AND SO I DUG RIGHT IN, HOPING TO FIND...*SOMETHING.*
OKAY.
HERE WE GO.
July 8th
Dear Diary,
I begin writing this on my 9th birthday. Within these pages, I will plumb the depths of my soul, and the world around me in a quest to find the meaning of life itself. My journey begins TOMORROW!
FLIP.
July 9th
My room smells like donkey butt! HA HA HA. Also, my foot really itches! I hope it's not the fungus again!
Tanner
I MAY BE IN TROUBLE.

'm not sure, but I think I hate school. Well, maybe not hate, but it sure is boring.

Today, we were reading one of the Spoingle book. The Spoingle is messed up, man.

Mrs. Hill called on Randy Gallagher to read out loud. UGH! Talk about boring! I think he even put Mrs. Hill to sleep. I thought about screaming at the top of my lungs just to see what would happen, but I decided against it.

No promises tomorrow though!

The good news is that Mikey (the boy who lives next door to us) said "Hi" to me three times today. I said "Hi" the first TWO of the times, but I don't care.... It still counts! He's so cute, I can barely stand it. I think he likes Mary more though. Big sisters are the WORST! She's never even nice to him. She calls him names I don't even UNDERSTAND!

Tanner

PS: On second thought, I do hate school!

PPS: At recess, Randy Gallagher asked if I wanted to play "doctor." I'm not sure what that means, but I kicked him in the shin, just to be safe.

Tanner

Today was the best and worst day EVER! Randy was bugging me ALL DAY. All he ever does is tease me. It's awful! Mary always says it's 'cause he likes me, but that makes no sense! If you like someone, just say "I like you"! Don't pull their pigtails till they cry. Plus, I get picked on a lot. Half the class calls me a freak, so either they ALL love me or they all really do think I'm a freak. But, you know what, I don't care. Because something awesome happened to me today.

On the way home, Randy was picking on me (of course) and he took my book bag. He was trying to throw it up in a tree! But Mikey saw and came over to stop it. AND GUESS WHAT? Randy beat the snot out of him!

Which I know sounds bad, right? But that means Mikey was willing to get beat up over ME!

Mary is still so dumb! She still thinks that Randy likes me and that Mikey was just being NICE! That makes no SENSE! Mary can be so stooooooooopid! If you like someone, you are nice. If you DON'T like someone, you are mean. END OF STORY!

Tanner

THE MAGAZINE WAS A LITTLE MORE INTERESTING....

Catching Up With... *Tanner Clark*

ANYONE FAMILIAR with the alt rock scene of the past few years knows the name *TANNER CLARK*. Her runaway hit album *Broken Record* and it's ubiquitous single "Gaberdine Prom Queen" made her the voice of a new generation of repressed, unappreciated suburban girls. But suddenly, at the height of her success, she vanished. Rumors of censorship, bankruptcy, and worse followed, but through it all, Clark remained silent. Recently, **On the Scene** caught up with Ms. Clark for a rare phone interview.

ROCKER
I MEAN, HEY, IT ALMOST SORTA MENTIONED ME!

The enigmatic Tanner Clark at an early club performance

On the Scene: So the music world is wondering where you disappeared to.
Tanner Clark: I've been around.

On the Scene: You haven't been visible.
Tanner Clark: Really? I'm invisible? That's so weird! I can usually see myself in the mirror.

On the Scene: I mean, you haven't been performing or recording lately.
Tanner Clark: I performed a song just last night.

On the Scene: In public?
Tanner Clark: To my niece, in her room.

On the Scene: And that's satisfying to you?
Tanner Clark: Sure.

On the Scene: As satisfying as playing to an arena full of fans?
Tanner Clark: In some ways it's more satisfying. I mean, when people show up for a concert, I'm not even sure why they are there, y'know? I don't know what they want from the experience.

On the Scene: But you do know with your niece?
Tanner Clark: Look, it's just that she was sad, y'know? Her life felt out of control, I sang her a song, and she felt better.

On the Scene: And that's all you need?
Tanner Clark: That's all I can give.

On the Scene: Now or forever?
Tanner Clark: I can't answer that right now.

On the Scene: Is there anything else you'd like to say to your fans?

Tanner Clark (long pause): Just...thank you, I guess. I never expected to have an audience or get to make a record....They made that possible...but nothing lasts forever, y'know? I just needed to run away for a while.

On the Scene: So you might be back someday?
Tanner Clark: I wish I could say yes, but I simply don't know.

On the Scene: But in the meantime, you'll play for your niece?
Tanner Clark: Yep.

On the Scene: Do you think, with all your talent, if that's what you gave to the world...one happy kid...would that be enough? I mean, with all you are capable of doing?

Tanner Clark: Not everything needs to be a grand gesture, y'know? And not every problem in life can be fixed with a song or a play or a book. Sometimes it's just the opposite. Sometimes the best way to get someone through the pain of their past or their present is just to be there with them and to hold their hand and wait for the future.

BUT IT REALLY WASN'T ANY MORE HELPFUL THAN THE

MAYBE I'LL HAVE BETTER LUCK WITH THE OTHER ONE.
FLIP FLIP FLIP
EMPTY.
HMM...
Dear Tanner,

I'm writing this in your old book. Maybe I'll show it to you someday. Maybe I won't. Honestly, I'm pretty mad at you right now. I've e-mailed you, like, a zillion times, and you never write back. I knew things would be different when you left, but I didn't think you'd forget about me. I guess you have, though, and that makes me feel stupid.

I guess I should be used to this by now. Nothing lasts. Nothing. Why should you be any different?

You know what's weird, though? I've noticed lately that when I'm feeling bad, I'm only mostly feeling bad. It's like there's a tiny part of me that almost enjoys it. Weird, I know, but it's true.

I noticed this a long time ago, but I've been thinking about it a lot lately. Anyway, I'm gonna write it all down in here, and someday, you'll read it and can tell me what you think.

Unless you never read it, because I never see you again, in which case, I don't care what you think.

Anyway...

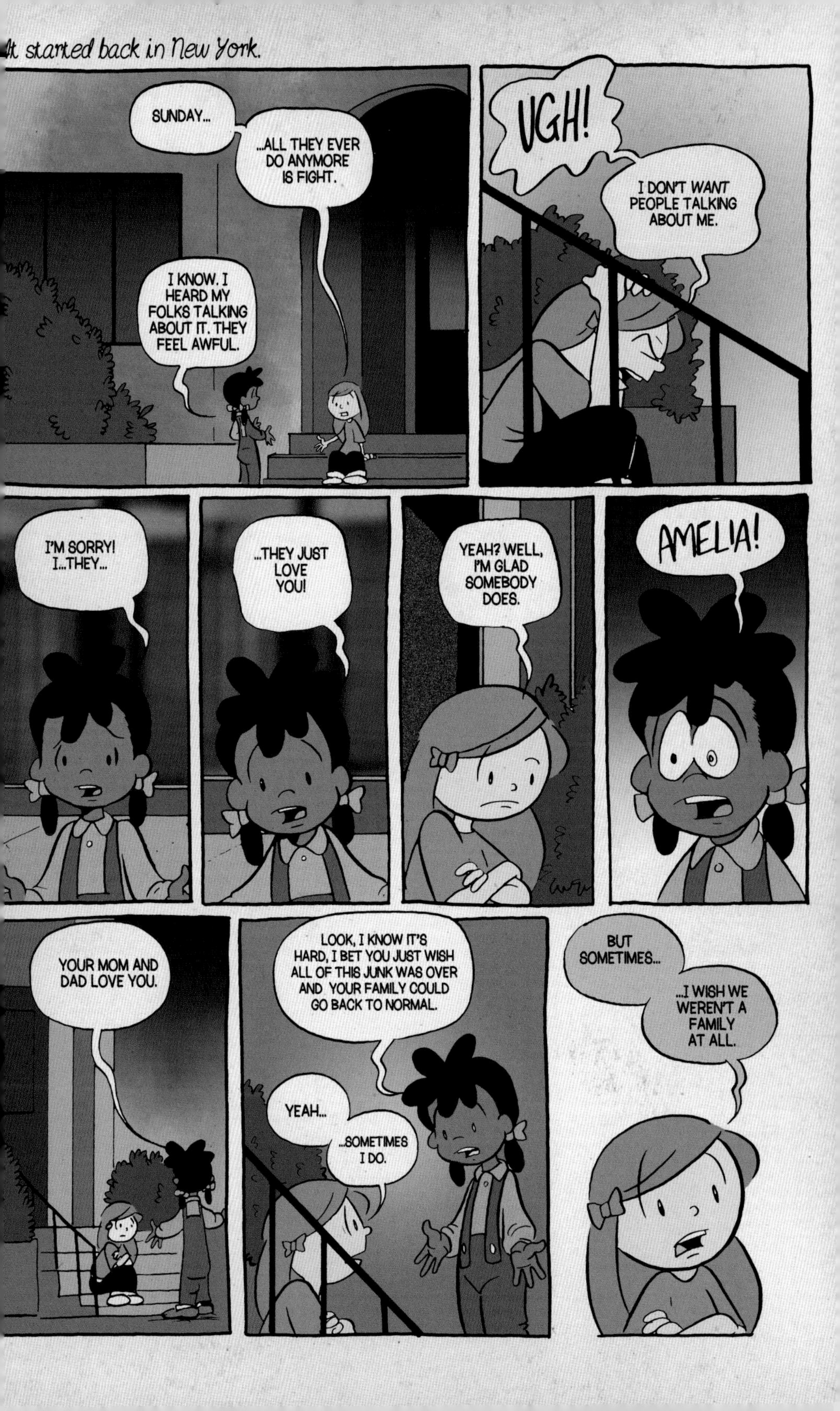
It started back in New York.
SUNDAY...
...ALL THEY EVER DO ANYMORE IS FIGHT.
I KNOW. I HEARD MY FOLKS TALKING ABOUT IT. THEY FEEL AWFUL.
UGH!
I DON'T WANT PEOPLE TALKING ABOUT ME.
I'M SORRY! I...THEY...
...THEY JUST LOVE YOU!
YEAH? WELL, I'M GLAD SOMEBODY DOES.
AMELIA!
YOUR MOM AND DAD LOVE YOU.
LOOK, I KNOW IT'S HARD, I BET YOU JUST WISH ALL OF THIS JUNK WAS OVER AND YOUR FAMILY COULD GO BACK TO NORMAL.
YEAH...
...SOMETIMES I DO.
BUT SOMETIMES...
...I WISH WE WEREN'T A FAMILY AT ALL.

HEY, GUYS! WANNA GO TO THE PARK?
OH GREAT! JUST WHAT I NEED! THE DWEEB KING.
AWW, KNOCK IT OFF, AMELIA!
YEAH, C'MON! IRA'S COOL!
I DON'T UNDERSTAND WHAT I DID TO GET YOU SO CHEESED OFF.
UH...YOU EXIST?
FORGET IT, IRA. MAYBE WE SHOULD JUST—
OKAY! OKAY!
I WAS ONLY TEASING!
LET'S GO TO THE STUPID PARK, IF THAT'S WHAT MAKES YOU HAPPY.
LOOK, AMELIA. IRA IS OUR FRIEND. SO YOU BETTER START—
RELAX, OKAY! I'LL BE NICE.
LOOK, I'M SMILING!

So we went over to the park. I was always supposed to tell Mom and Dad if I left the front of the building, but I didn't care.

It was one of those days when it feels like it will rain any second...

...only it never does.

Sunday and Ira were playing hide-and-seek, but I didn't feel like playing.

I just sat there, all hunkered down. My eyes were almost closed, and I was just, I don't know, feeling my anger.

It was like a big ball of blackness inside me, and I liked it.

Eventually, Ira and Sunday got sick of their two-person game of hide-and-seek, and they realized I was in no mood to play. So we all started walking home.
SIGH WELL, THAT WAS...
..."FUN."
OH, YEAH...
...A BLAST.
WELL, MAYBE IF YOU WOULD'VE PLAYED A LITTLE....
OH, FORGET IT, SUNDAY.
WHAT FUN IS PLAYING...
...WHEN YOU CAN SPEND THE DAY BEING A JERK!
SMACK!

And that was the worst thing that I ever did.
And when people like Principal Wright say that I'm bad, I remember that moment...
and I worry they might be right.

BAD?!
WHY, YOU'RE NOTHING BUT A SMALL NUISANCE, NINJA! A FLY IN THE OINTMENT!
DO YOU BELIEVE YOU CAN CHALLENGE MY POWER?
YOU FOOL!
MY POWER IS THE POWER OF RIGHTEOUSNESS!
WHILE YOURS REMAINS BUT TRICKERY!
YOU CALL THIS TRICKERY, HERO?!
!!
POW
?!
AHH!

OW!
?
BWAAA!
!!
I'M TELLING MY MOMMY!!
FINE!
AND TELL HER CAPTAIN AMAZING SHALL ALWAYS DEFEAT HER EVIL BROOD!
AND THAT'S HOW G.A.S.P. VANQUISHED THE NINJAS AT THE BATTLE OF PARK VIEW TERRACE.
WOW!

SIGH
IT'S JUST SUCH A SHAME ABOUT THE CLUBHOUSE.
IT SHOULD STAND FOREVER AS A MONUMENT TO THE AWESOME FEATS OF G.A.S.P.
YEAH...
...WE WERE PRETTY AWESOME.
IF ONLY ONE OF US HAD A SUPERBRAIN, WE COULD—
?!
SPACEMONKEYS!
I JUST THOUGHT OF SOMETHING!
MY COUSIN IS THE SMARTEST KID I KNOW! HE COULD FIX THIS, NO PROBLEM!
YEAH, THAT'S IT!
I WON'T FAIL YOU, SIR!
GOOD LUCK, KID!
YOOOOOO COMPLEEEETE MEEEE!
KAPWANG!
WOOOOSH!

AND SO, ABOUT FIFTEEN MINUTES LATER...
HOWEVER, WHEN WE CONCEIVE OF SPACE TIME AS AN ALMOST UNIMAGINABLY LARGE FOUR-DIMENSIONAL SOLID...
...WHICH CONTAINS NOT ONLY EVERY MOMENT THAT EVER *WAS* OR EVER *WILL* BE...
...BUT *ALSO* CONTAINS EVERY MOMENT THAT *COULD* HAVE BEEN, AND WHICH *MAY YET* BE...
...WE CAN DEDUCE THAT IT IS HUMAN CONSCIOUSNESS MOVING THROUGH THIS CONSTRUCT THAT CREATES OUR PERCEPTION OF TIME... OF CHOICE...
...AND THEREFORE, WE CAN CONCLUSIVELY PROVE THAT FREE WILL CAN EXIST HARMONIOUSLY IN AN EINSTEINIAN UNIVERSE!
UH... AND JUNK LIKE THAT.
ARE THERE UH...
...ANY QUESTIONS?
JUST ONE.
CAN YOU **FIX** THE CLUBHOUSE OR **NOT**?
YES.
BUT IT'LL COST ABOUT FIFTY BUCKS.

GREAT!
IT'S A DEAL!
C'MON, KID AMAZING. WE HAVE A MISSION.
OOH! WHAT'S THAT?!
YOU HAVE TO FIND US FIFTY BUCKS.
WOW!
IT WILL BE AN *HONOR* TO HIT UP MY PARENTS, SIR!
SO, TURNIP BRAIN, DO YOU REALLY THINK YOU CAN FIX THE CLUBHOUSE?
SURE.
WHY NOT?
WELL, IT'S BROKEN PRETTY BAD.
AND SOMETIMES THINGS GET SO BROKEN, THEY CAN NEVER BE FIXED.
WELL, THAT'S TRUE, I GUESS.
BUT SCIENCE TELLS US THAT NOTHING CAN TRULY BE CREATED OR DESTROYED.
SO MAYBE THIS *CAN'T* BE PUT BACK TOGETHER...
...BUT WHEN THAT HAPPENS...
...YOU PICK UP THE PIECES AND MAKE SOMETHING NEW.

OKAY...
...BEFORE MOM AND I LEFT NEW YORK, I SAW A DOCTOR ABOUT THE PROBLEM I WAS HAVING.
THIS IS WHAT HE TOLD ME:
SOMETIMES, A THING IS BROKEN SO BADLY, THERE'S NO WAY TO PUT IT BACK TOGETHER.
BUT NOW HERE'S TURNIP BRAIN SAYING:
IF YOU CAN'T PUT SOMETHING BACK TOGETHER, PICK UP THE PIECES AND MAKE SOMETHING NEW.
Y'KNOW, I THINK MR. HENDERSON IS RIGHT. THERE *IS* SOMETHING HOLIDING ME BACK.
AND IT'S NOT THAT PRINCIPAL WRIGHT THINKS THAT I'M BAD.
IT'S THAT DEEP DOWN INSIDE...
I *AGREE* WITH HIM.
THAT WEEKEND, MY DAD WAS GOING TO NEW YORK TO COLLECT THE LAST OF HIS THINGS AND OFFICIALLY PUT OUR OLD PLACE UP FOR SALE.
HE ASKED IF I WANTED TO GO, AND AT FIRST I SAID NO. I DIDN'T WANT TO SEE OUR APARTMENT ALL EMPTY AND SAD.
BUT THEN I DECIDED TO CHANGE MY MIND.
I HAD A SCIENTIFIC THEORY TO TEST.

SEEING THE APARTMENT WAS WORSE THAN I THOUGHT.
I GUESS HAVING MOM AND DAD TOGETHER SO MUCH LATELY (AND NOT EVEN FIGHTING!) MADE ME FORGET ALL THAT HAD HAPPENED.
BUT THIS... THIS BROUGHT IT ALL BACK.
SCORE ONE FOR THE "CAN'T BE FIXED" THEORY.
HEY!
?
HEY, SUNDAY!
I GOT YOUR TEXT.
WOW.

THIS IS DEPRESSING!
I KNOW, BUT FORGET IT RIGHT NOW.
I HAVE SOMETHING I NEED TO DO, AND I WANT YOU TO COME ALONG.
SUNDAY! GOOD TO SEE YOU.
HOW'S YOUR DAD?
HE'S GOOD!
HE'S UPSTAIRS RIGHT NOW, YOU SHOULD GO SAY HI.
HMM...I'D LOVE TO! BUT WE DON'T HAVE A LOT OF--
GO AHEAD, DAD!
YOU LOVE HANGING OUT WITH MR. JONES, AND WHO KNOWS WHEN WE'LL BE BACK IN THE CITY?
DON'T WORRY. SUNDAY AND I CAN KEEP OURSELVES BUSY.
?

I FILLED SUNDAY IN ON MY PLAN, AND BEFORE ^ KNEW IT, WE WERE DOWN THE ELEVATOR, OUT THE LOBBY, AND ZOOMING UP THE STREET— TERRORIZING ALL THE PEDESTRIANS LIKE WE ALWAYS DID.
IT FELT LIKE IT ALWAYS DID. LIKE IT USED TO, WHICH WAS GREAT, BECAUSE I KNEW IT WOULD NEVER HAPPEN AGAIN.

IS THIS CRAZY?
THIS IS CRAZY, RIGHT?
WE'LL FIND OUT IN A SECOND.

WHEN IRA OPENED THE DOOR, I ALMOST GASPED! HE LOOKED SO . . . DIFFERENT!

HE DIDN'T SAY ANYTHING, SO I JUST LAUNCHED RIGHT INTO MY APOLOGY.

I TOLD HIM I WAS SORRY FOR HITTING HIM. I WAS SORRY FOR BEING A JERK. I WAS SORRY FOR GOING SO LONG WITHOUT SAYING SORRY.

AND THEN, EVEN THOUGH I REALLY DIDN'T WANT TO, I STARTED TO CRY.

I GUESS I WAS MAKING A SCENE, BECAUSE IRA'S MOM CAME TO THE DOOR...

301
WELCOME
FRIENDS
...AND BROUGHT US ALL INSIDE.

LOVE!
LIFE
FRIENDSHIP
TRUTH
CANDY MAKING 101
BEAUTY

AFTER I GOT HOME, I WAS BACK TO READING TANNER'S OLD DIARIES. YOU CAN IMAGINE MY SURPRISE WHEN I FOUND OUT THE LITTLE BOY TANNER USED TO MOON OVER...

I found out today that Mikey McBride is moving. What worse is we're suppose to visit my aunt Sarah in Pen sylvania and by the time we get back, he'll be gone.

I don't even want to go see Aunt Sarah. She's so dumb She writes these kids' books and they're cool and all, b she doesn't even sign her own name. So she's not eve famous. PLUS, instead of living some place cool, like New York or Paris, she lives in some dumb town in Pennsylvania. I swear, if that ever happens to me, I hope somebody puts me out of my misery. AAGH!

I'm gonna miss Mikey. He was always nice and never called me a weirdo like everyone else. Mary's so dumb. Mikey totally liked her and she was never ever nice to him.

UPDATE: Get this: I told Mary that Mikey was moving and she cried! Are you kidding me?? She does nothing but tease him and call him names and the minute she finds out he won't be around, she loses it. I WILL NEVER UNDERSTAND PEOPLE! EVER!

...WAS MY *DAD!*

Tanner

OBVIOUSLY, THIS NEEDED TO BE DISCUSSED....
I SWEAR!
SHE HAD A FULL ON CRUSH...
...ON MY DAD!
THIS IS SUPER WEIRD.
WELL, BIG DEAL! SHE WAS A LITTLE KID...
...YOUNGER THAN WE ARE NOW!
I KNOW! I KNOW!
BUT CAN YOU JUST IMAGINE?!
YEAH! TANNER COULD HAVE BEEN...
!
...YOUR MOM!
whoa.
Y'KNOW, I BET THE GROWN-UP ME WOULD HAVE HAD A ROCKIN' BOD.
I WAS GONNA SAY!

HEY, I'M GONNA GO HELP MY MOM MAKE MORE BON BOMBS. WANNA HELP?
UGH! NO!
LAST TIME I HELPED, I ATE LIKE FORTY!
ME TOO!
AND THEN I HAD A DREAM I WAS DROWING IN THE CREAMY COOKIE FILLING, AND I HAD TO EAT MY WAY TO SAFETY.
IT WAS THE BEST DREAM I EVER HAD.
SIIIIIIIIIIIGH
HEY, RHONDA, AFTER MY MEETING, WE SHOULD GO OVER TO REGGIE'S.
SORRY, MY CAPE IS IN THE WASH.
C'MON, YOU NEVER HANG OUT WITH HIM ANYMORE.
DOES HE MISS ME?
OF COURSE!

GOOD.

BUT I DON'T UNDERSTAND! IF SHE MADE THE TEAM, THEN...
YES, BUT MR. McBRIDE, THE ENTIRE POINT OF THESE MEETINGS IS TO KEEP YOUR DAUGHTER ON THE CORRECT PATH.
JOE McCARTHY ELEMENTARY
"Weeding out the wrong element since 1952"
BUT YOU SAID SHE WAS IMPROVING.
IMPROVING, YES.
BUT SHE'S NOT THERE YET.
MAYBE NEXT YEAR.
YOU UNDERSTAND, DON'T YOU AMELIA?
I-
UMM...EXCUSE ME.

PRINCIPAL WRIGHT? I'M SORRY TO INTERRUPT.
BUT I WANTED TO TURN IN MY UNIFORM.
!
AMELIA MADE THE TEAM FAIR AND SQUARE.
AND I DON'T THINK IT'S RIGHT FOR YOU TO KEEP HER OFF.
SO IF AMELIA CAN'T BE ON THE TEAM, I DON'T WANT TO BE ON THE TEAM EITHER.
I'VE SPOKEN TO ALL THE OTHER GIRLS, AND THEY FEEL THE SAME WAY.
SO IF AMELIA'S NOT ON THE TEAM, THEN I GUESS THERE IS NO TEAM.

WOOOO-HOOOO!!
DID YOU SEE HOW FAST HE BACKED DOWN?
RHONDA! THAT WAS AMAZING!
HONEY! STICKING UP FOR YOUR FRIEND LIKE THAT! THAT WAS SO BRAVE!
AWW. IT WAS NOTHING.
FORGET IT!
MAN! I'VE NEVER SEEN YOUR PARENTS ACTING SO GOOFY.
YEAH.
I CAN'T BELIEVE ALL THOSE GIRLS WERE WILLING TO QUIT FOR ME.
THEY WEREN'T! ARE YOU KIDDING? I WAS BLUFFING!
WHAT?
THEN WHY?
THE FIRST THING BRITNEY SAID TO ME AT OUR FIRST PRACTICE WAS THAT YOU HAD GIVEN YOUR SPOT UP FOR ME.
RHONDA, I—
AMEALIA, THANK YOU.

NOW WE'RE EVEN.

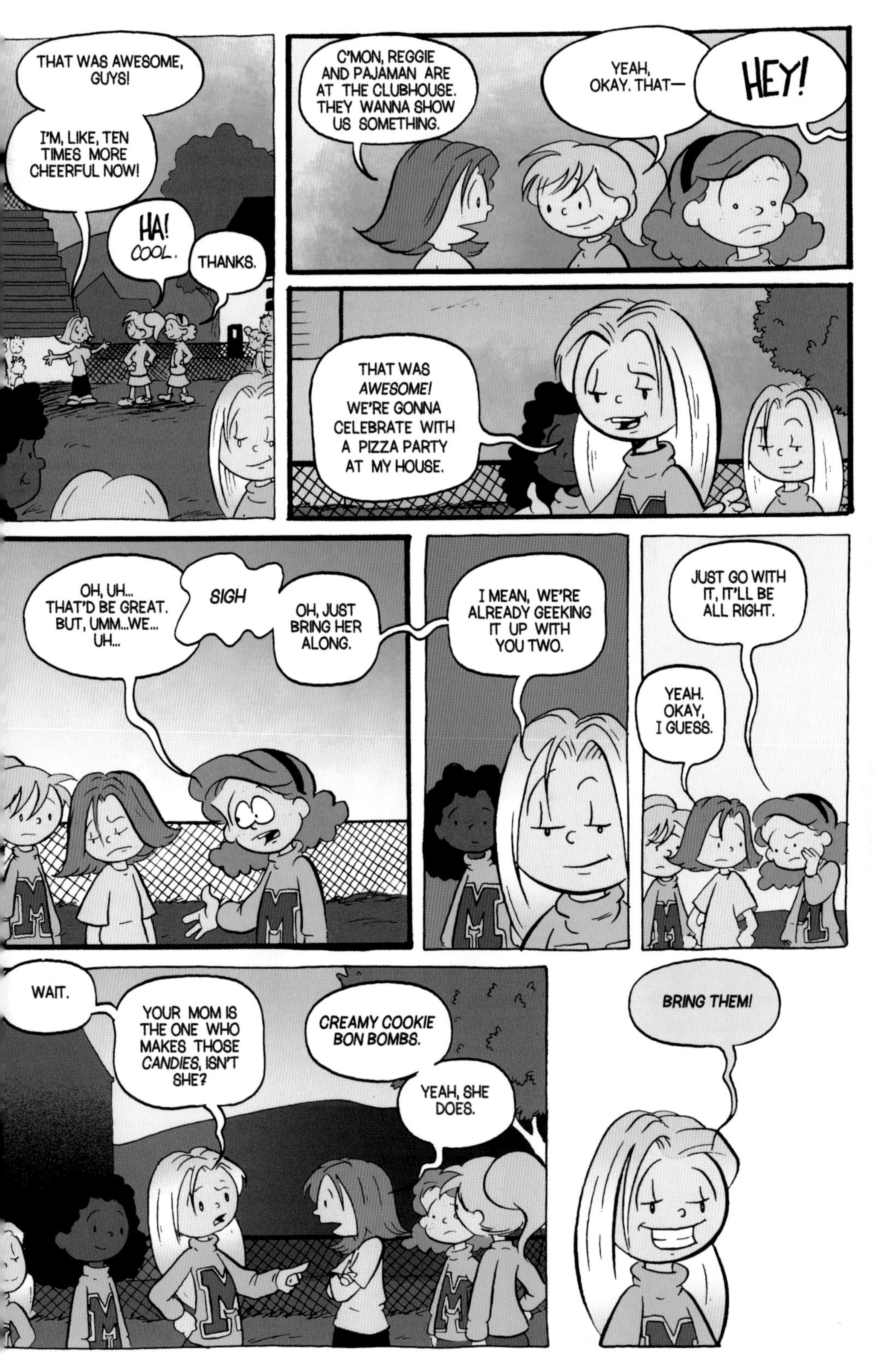
THAT WAS AWESOME, GUYS!
I'M, LIKE, TEN TIMES MORE CHEERFUL NOW!
HA! COOL.
THANKS.
C'MON, REGGIE AND PAJAMAN ARE AT THE CLUBHOUSE. THEY WANNA SHOW US SOMETHING.
YEAH, OKAY. THAT—
HEY!
THAT WAS AWESOME! WE'RE GONNA CELEBRATE WITH A PIZZA PARTY AT MY HOUSE.
OH, UH... THAT'D BE GREAT. BUT, UMM...WE... UH...
SIGH
OH, JUST BRING HER ALONG.
I MEAN, WE'RE ALREADY GEEKING IT UP WITH YOU TWO.
JUST GO WITH IT, IT'LL BE ALL RIGHT.
YEAH. OKAY, I GUESS.
WAIT.
YOUR MOM IS THE ONE WHO MAKES THOSE CANDIES, ISN'T SHE?
CREAMY COOKIE BON BOMBS.
YEAH, SHE DOES.
BRING THEM!

BRING LOTS OF THEM.

HUH?
WHAT DOES THAT MEAN?
OH, THAT'S GEEK FOR "SHE WANTED TO KICK YOUR BUTT."
WHAT?!
I AM SHOCKED!
AND AFTER ALL I'VE DONE FOR YOU!
?
WHAT DID YOU EVER DO FOR ME?
HEY! IT WAS MY... "CONSTRUCTIVE CRITICISM" THAT INSPIRED YOU TO IMPROVE YOURSELF.
IF IT WASN'T FOR ME, YOU'D STILL BE RUNNING AROUND PLAYING "SUPERHERO."
HEY! LISTEN...
SORRY, I'M BORED NOW.
HEY, YOU.
ME?
YEAH.
WHAT'S YOUR STORY?

MY STORY?
YOU'RE NEW TO OUR SCHOOL, RIGHT?
YEAH. I USED TO GO TO ST. JOE'S.
BUT MY DAD'S IN THE ARMY AND HE GOT DEPLOYED–
WHOA!
THE ARMY!
IS HE, LIKE, FIGHTING PEOPLE WITH, LIKE, BOMBS AND STUFF?
ARE WE EVEN FIGHTING SOMEONE NOW?
DUH, BRITNEY!
WE'RE ALWAYS FIGHTING SOMEBODY.
WHEN'S HE COMING HOME?
IN A FEW MONTHS... BUT IT FEELS LIKE HE'S BEEN GONE FOREVER.
WELL, MAYBE HE'LL GET TO COME HOME EARLY.
NO!
NO. DON'T SAY THAT! THAT WOULD ONLY BE BAD.
REALLY BAD.

LAST NIGHT I HAD THIS DREAM.
I WAS SUPPOSED TO MEET HIM.
I LOOKED EVERYWHERE AND COULDN'T FIND HIM.
I ENDED UP FLOATING IN THE OCEAN, JUST LOST, AND CRYING.
AND I WAS ALL ALONE.
ANYWAY...
IT'S JUST A STUPID DREAM, RIGHT? THEY DON'T MEAN ANYTHING.
YEAH.
YOU PROBABLY JUST ATE SOMETHING WEIRD.
Y'KNOW HOW THAT GOES.
RIGHT, YOU PROBABLY GORGED ON THESE CANDIES.
IF MY MOM MADE THEM, THEY'D NEED A CRANE TO GET ME OUT OF MY HOUSE.
ACTUALLY, I'VE SEEN THE REST OF YOUR FAMILY.
THERE'S A GOOD CHANCE THAT WILL HAPPEN ANYWAY.
!

Y'KNOW WHAT?
YOU *ARE* A NIGHTMARE.
Y'KNOW? THAT WENT AMAZINGLY WELL!
I KNOW! THEY *WERE EVEN ALMOST* NICE TO JOAN!
YEAH, RIGHT?
HEH
I GUESS THE CANDY HELPED.
TOO BAD SHE HAD TO LEAVE EARLY.
YEAH.
HER MOM SEEMED PRETTY WORKED UP.
HEY!
OH, HEY GUYS!
WHAT'S UP?
"WHAT'S UP?!"
I INVITED YOU GUYS OVER.
I KNOW JOAN TOLD YOU. I WATCHED HER!
YOU JUST BLEW ME OFF.

REGGIE, C'MON. YOU KNOW WE DIDN'T—
!
HEY!
THE CLUBHOUSE!
TURNIP BRAIN AND THOSE LITTLE KIDS FINISHED IT.
IT LOOKS JUST THE SAME!

OH, YEAH?
LOOK INSIDE.
?
!
IS THAT A—
YES, IT IS.
DOES IT WORK?
YES, IT DOES.
WHOA.
OH, C'MON! WHAT DO YOU CARE?

REGGIE! WE'RE SORRY, OKAY? BRITNEY INVITED US TO—
BRITNEY!?
RHONDA! BRITNEY HATES YOU! SHE HATES AMELIA!
SHE IS EVIL!
REGGIE, C'MON. YOU'RE BEING A JERK!
OH, YEAH?
WELL, I'M NOT THE ONE WHO FORGOT ABOUT YOU.
AMELIA...
...I HAVE ONE OF MY OLD COSTUMES AT YOUR HOUSE. I WANT TO GO AND GET IT BACK.
AWW, REGGIE...
...COME ON...
...PLEASE?
AMELIA, THERE'S NOTHING LEFT TO SAY.

WHEN WE GOT TO MY HOUSE, MY MOM WAS WAITING FOR US. AT FIRST I THOUGHT SHE WAS JUST OUT ENJOYING THE BEAUTIFUL WEATHER. BUT WHEN WE GOT CLOSER, I COULD SEE SHE LOOKED AWFUL, LIKE SHE WAS SICK— LIKE SHE'D SEEN A GHOST.

I STARTED CRYING, Y'KNOW? JUST BAWLING LIKE A BABY.
MY MOM GRABBED ME AND HELD ME SO TIGHT IT HURT. FINALLY, THROUGH THE SOUND OF MY OWN MELTDOWN, I STARTED TO HEAR HER VOICE AGAIN.
WUHUHUHUH HUHUHUHUH
...HAVEN'T FOUND ANY SURVIVORS, OR... CASUALTIES.
THEY SAID THEY'RE STILL SEARCHING.
!!
THEN HE COULD STILL BE ALIVE?
OH, HONEY... ...IT'S JUST SO...
...WELL...I GUESS WE SHOULD TRY TO HOPE.
JOAN...HER... HER MOM SAID SHE NEEDS HER FRIENDS.
BUT LISTEN, THIS IS GROWN-UP STUFF.
I'M SURE SHE'D UNDERSTAND IF YOU CAN'T—
NO!

WE NEED TO GO TO HER.
C'MON LET'S—
!
WHERE'S PAJAMAMAN?
HE TOOK OFF!
I THINK HE'S ON HIS WAY.
OKAY C'MON, RHONDA, LET'S...
RHONDA?
I...
...I CAN'T
WHY...
WHAT DO YOU MEAN?
I CAN'T DO IT!
I DON'T KNOW WHAT TO SAY!
I MEAN HER DAD COULD BE-
RHONDA!
YOU'RE SUCH A...
...

LOOK, RHONDA, WHY DID YOU GIVE UP YOUR SPOT AS A CHEERLEADER?
WHY DID I GIVE UP MY SPOT FOR YOU?
BECAUSE...
...BECAUSE WE'RE FRIENDS.
...AND BECAUSE I LOVE YOU, YOU IDIOT.
MAN, I *HATE* YOU.
WELL, WHAT ABOUT JOAN?
REGGIE, I'M REALLY SCARED.
WILL YOU HOLD MY HAND?
OH!
OH...SURE.
OF *COURSE!*

I WISH I COULD SAY WE RAN BRAVELY OVER TO JOAN'S, BUT WE DIDN'T.

WITH EVERY STEP, I WANTED TO TURN AROUND AND RUN HOME, AND I KNOW THE OTHERS FELT THE SAME.

HONESTLY, WE BARELY MADE IT.

JOAN?
I KNEW IT WAS GOING TO HAPPEN.
I KNEW IT.
I THOUGHT ABOUT IT HAPPENING SO OFTEN THAT WHEN IT DID, IT WAS LIKE DÉJÀ VU.
JOAN, C'MON.
HE...
HE COULD STILL BE ALIVE.
JOAN...
......
W-What...
WHAT DO YOU NEED US TO DO?
PLEASE,
JUST BE HERE...

WHENEVER PRINCIPAL WRIGHT TELLS ME SOMETHING I DON'T WANT TO HEAR, HE ASKS ME...
..."DO YOU UNDERSTAND?"
I ALWAYS SAY "YES." BUT Y'KNOW WHAT?
I *DON'T* UNDERSTAND.
I'M SURE THERE IS A VERY GROWN-UP REASON WHY JOAN'S DAD IS MISSING ON THE OTHER SIDE OF THE WORLD.
AND I'M SURE GROWN-UPS LIKE PRINCIPAL WRIGHT KNOW WHAT THAT REASON IS.
BUT IF I ASKED THEM TO EXPLAIN IT TO ME, THEY WOULDN'T. BECAUSE I'M "JUST A KID."
BUT THAT DOESN'T CHANGE THE FACT THAT JOAN'S DAD MIGHT BE DEAD.
OR THAT I HAVE NO IDEA WHAT TO SAY TO HER.

WHEN I SAW MY PARENTS REACT TO RHONDA QUITTING THE TEAM FOR ME...
...IT WAS LIKE THEY WERE STILL THE LITTLE KIDS FROM TANNER'S DIARY.
BUT THEY'RE SUPPOSE TO BE GROWN-UPS, AND I AM A KID, AND I FEEL LIKE I'M A HUNDRED.
AND Y'KNOW WHAT? I MAY NEVER KNOW THE MEANING OF LIFE, BUT I DO KNOW THIS...
...THERE IS NO SUCH THING AS A "KID WORLD" OR AN "ADULT WORLD."
IN REALITY, THERE'S JUST ONE WORLD.
IN REALITY, WE'RE PRAYING FOR THE PHONE TO RING.

LOOK, IF WE'RE GOING TO BE A *REAL* TEAM, WE HAVE TO SWEAR LOYALTY.
WELL, I'LL TELL YOU RIGHT NOW, I'M NOT DOING THE WHOLE "BLOOD BROTHER" THING.
BECAUSE *ONE:* I'M A GIRL.
TWO: I'M AFRAID OF POINTY THINGS.
AND *THREE*: I DON'T KNOW WHERE HER BLOOD HAS BEEN.
FINE. HOW ABOUT WE SPIT SWEAR?
EEEW! I DON'T KNOW WHERE YOUR SPIT'S BEEN EITHER!
WE'LL JUST PINKY SWEAR, OKAY?
THAT PART DOESN'T MATTER....
ALL THAT MATTERS IS THAT WE'RE IN THIS TOGETHER NOW...
...*FOREVER*...
...AND NO MATTER WHAT TRIALS, WHAT CHALLENGES, WHAT EVIL IS THROWN AT US...

...THEY WILL NEVER
TEAR US APART.

RRRIIIING
ALIVE!!
OH, THANKGOD, THANKGOD, THANKGOD!
YES. WILL HE BE OKAY?
YES. NO, I UNDERSTAND! WHEN? YES...

A SEVERE CONCUSSION. A BROKEN WRIST. A BROKEN LEG...
...AND THAT WAS CONSIDERED *GOOD* NEWS.
THE WORLD IS SCARY SOMETIMES.
BUT NOTHING LASTS, Y'KNOW? NOT EVEN THE BAD STUFF.
DAYS TURNED TO WEEKS, AND BEFORE WE KNEW IT, THE BLOCK PARTY WAS HERE.
AND THE WHOLE TOWN CELEBRATED THE FACT THAT WE EXISTED.
...A NICE ROUND OF APPLAUSE FOR...
...the JOE McCARTHY CHEERLEADERS!
AND NOW, A SPECIAL *BICENTENNIAL SURPRISE*!

CONNERTON, P.A.'S MOST FAMOUS DAUGHTER...
...MISS TANNER CLARK!
YEAH WOO HOO
HOORAY
!
THANK YOU! THANKS, EVERYONE!
IT'S GREAT TO BE BACK HOME, AND IT'S GREAT TO SEE THAT THE MORE THINGS CHANGE...
!
...WELL, THE MORE THINGS CHANGE, I GUESS!

AT FIRST, I WAS JUST SO BUSY, Y'KNOW?
TOURING, PLAYING IN FRONT OF PEOPLE, PLAYING SONGS I'D NEVER PLAYED BEFORE.
IT WAS JUST TOO MUCH.
THEN WEEKS PASSED, AND I FELT LIKE IT WAS TOO LATE TO WRITE. I FIGURED YOU ALREADY HATED ME.
ANYWAY, I'M SORRY.
I WON'T LEAVE YOU HANGING AGAIN.
THAT'S OKAY. WE'RE COOL.
WELL, I KNOW *THAT*, SILLY.
BY THE WAY, I READ YOUR DIARY.
!

OH, WELL...
I'M AN OPEN BOOK ANYWAY.
DID YOU EVER FIND IT?
?
FIND WHAT?
"THE MEANING OF LIFE."
OH!
HEH...RIGH.
NO, BUT I'LL KEEP YOU UPDATED.
HOLD ON... "MEANING OF LIFE"!
WAIT! WHICH DIARY DID YOU READ?
Oh, Mikey! He's Sooooooooo Cuuute!
OooooH!
SEE, NOW I HAVE TO DESTROY YOU.

HEY, SPEAKING OF "CUTE."
THERE'S YOUR BOYFRIEND.
OH, YEAH.
HE IS A CUTIE.
OH, GROSS! THAT IS MY TEACHER YOU'RE TALKING ABOUT, Y'KNOW?
OH, YEAH.
BY THE WAY, SORRY IF THAT WAS AWKWARD.
NAH, NOBODY CARED.
BUT I'LL TELL YOU WHAT, FOR ALL THE SMOOCHIN' YOU GUYS DID, IT DIDN'T MAKE HIM CUT ME ANY SLACK GRADE-WISE.
NO?
WELL, I GUESS I'LL HAVE TO SMOOCH HIM HARDER.
SIGH
KIDS TODAY.

OKAY. MAYBE NO ONE KNOWS THE "MEANING OF LIFE."
MAYBE NO ONE EVER WILL, BECAUSE PEOPLE ARE TOO WEIRD AND CRAZY AND STUPID.
BUT THERE ARE LOTS OF THINGS I'VE LEARNED. IMPORTANT THINGS THAT PEOPLE HAVE TAUGHT ME.
AND THERE ARE OTHER THINGS I'VE FIGURED OUT FOR MYSELF.
AND Y'KNOW WHAT?

FOR RIGHT NOW, THAT'S ENOUGH.
On the Scene: Do you think, with all your talent, if that's what you gave to the world...one happy kid...would that b enough? I mean, with all you are capable of doing?
Tanner Clark: Not everything needs to be a grand gesture, y'know?
And not every problem in life can be fixed with a song or a play or a book.
Sometimes it's just the opposite.

Sometimes the best way to get someone through the pain of their past or their present is just to be there with them

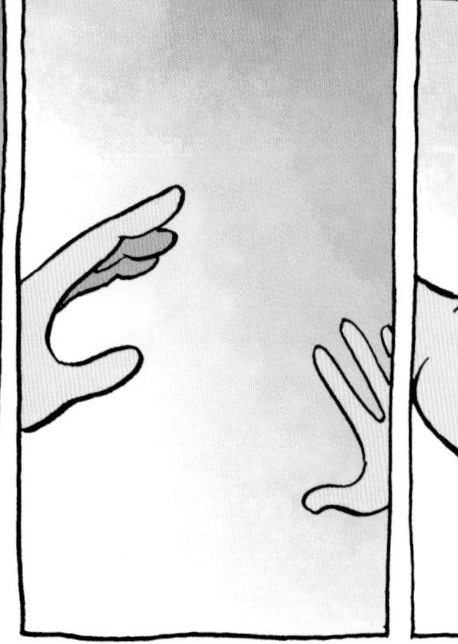
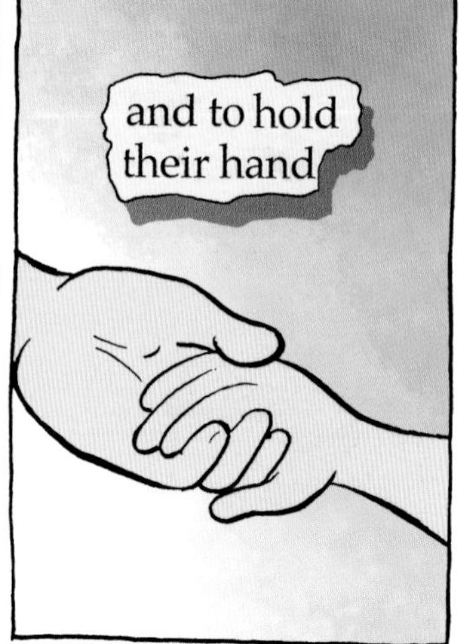

and wait for the future.

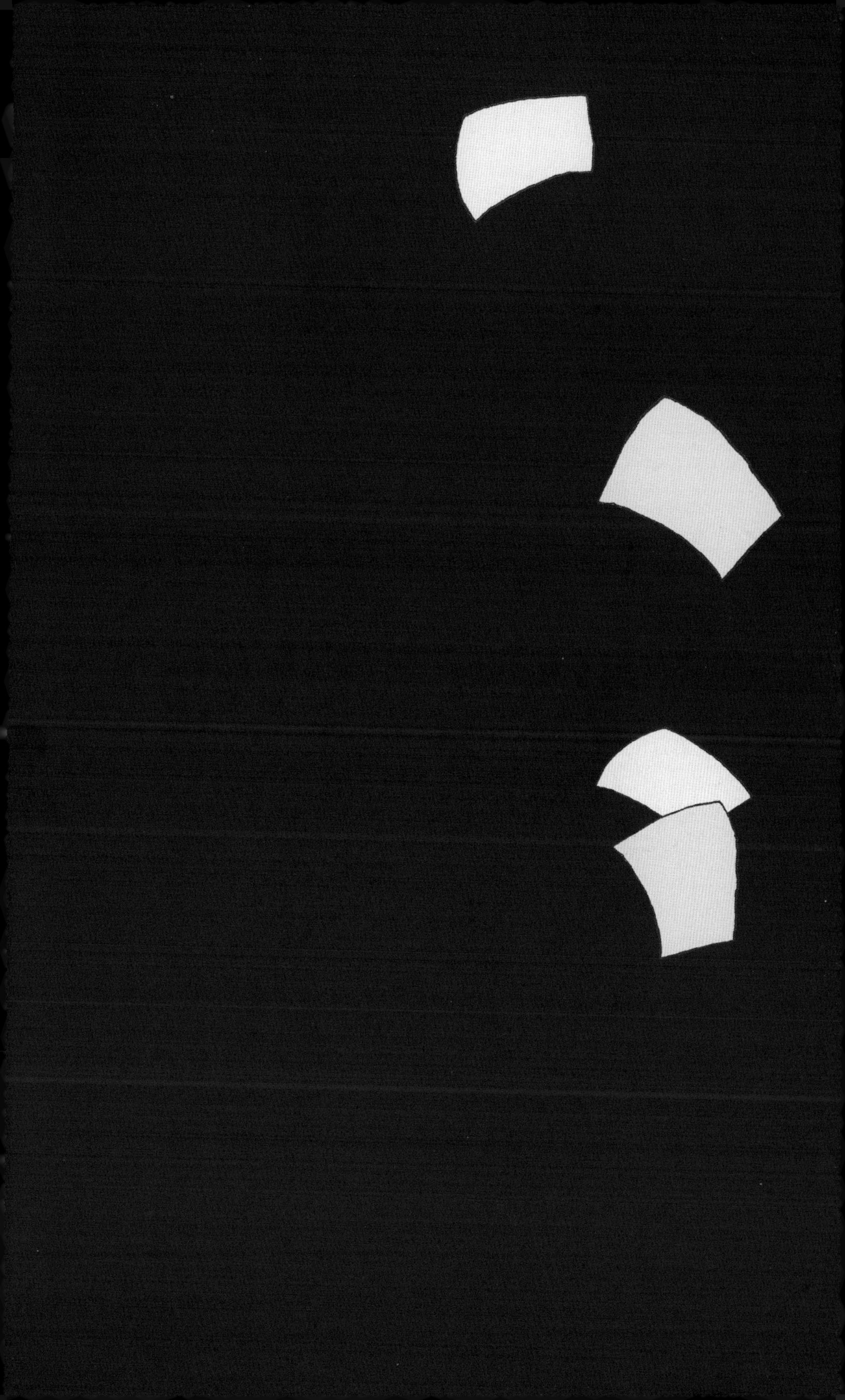

Jimmy Gownley's
AMELIA RULES!
Join Amelia and the gang for adventures, mishaps, and homework.
Collect them all!
THE WHOLE WORLD'S CRAZY
WHAT MAKES YOU HAPPY
SUPERHEROES
WHEN THE PAST IS A PRESENT
THE TWEENAGE GUIDE TO NOT BEING UNPOPULAR
TRUE THINGS (ADULTS DON'T WANT KIDS TO KNOW)
THE MEANING OF LIFE... AND OTHER STUFF
HER PERMANENT RECORD
BUS STOP
Jimmy Gownley